Kameleona/Chameleon
By Judith Fabris

Kameleona Chameleon

By Judith Fabris

VALDESOL PRESS
PALM SPRINGS, CA

The copyrighted kukui-nut quilt image that decorates each chapter was created by Jule Patten Kamakana. The ancient Hawaiians use the kukui or candlenut plant for food, as a candle, a wood for canoes, for many varieties of medicines, as a protective stain for fishing nets, and as an ornament for a kukui nut lei. The artist designed this kapa in honor of Lanikhula, a powerful kahuna (person of knowledge). He is buried in a grove of kukui trees named for him on Molokai's eastern cliffs.

Cover hibiscus quilt block image (c) Jule Patten Kamakana
Back cover photo: Clark Dugger Photography
Published by Valdesol Press, Palm Springs, CA

ISBN-10: 0-9860952-8-1
ISBN-13: 978-0-9860952-8-3

Dedication

To all my wonderful friends on Molokai, a place where each day that yellow ball of fire turns an emerald green before it sinks into a glassy ocean, the legendary birthplace of the goddess of hula as well as Kalaupapa, a place where people at one time were exiled for leprosy, now called Hansen's disease. It is now part of the National Park System.

*Thou wilt be condemned
into everlasting redemption for this.*

Shakespeare

Much Ado about Nothing

MOLOKAI

Papohaku
Beach

HOOLEHUA

MAUNALOA

Church of Good News

KAUNAKAKAI

Wharf

Molokai Forest Reserve

Halawa
Valley

HALAWA

Chapter One

Singapore, the Lion City

Jack stood in the shadows of an alley on Maxwell Road, long after the street hawkers left for the night. Escaping from the casino, he managed to evade the cartel's enforcers who had been following him. "It's not my fault the drug deal went south," he muttered to himself. Jack noticed a freighter in port that afternoon, and his plan called for him to board it and sail as part of the crew. *It's got to be heading for Hawaii.*

A young woman wearing a polka-dot cheongsam stood under the light of a dull street lamp. Jack figured she had just come from work, noting her white high heels and white earrings. He watched as four men in their early twenties approached her. When she shook her head no, the gang took matters into their own hands. Knocking her down to the ground, the first man tore her dress and panties, his fly already undone, ready to mount her while two other men held her arms down. The fourth man stood at the side as lookout. She screamed when one of the men hit her. Jack knew he couldn't stand by and let these hoods rape her.

Gun drawn on the leader, he walked out into their midst. "Let the girl alone. I'll shoot."

"Just try it. It'll be four against one." He stood up from where he had been on top of the girl.

Jack's bullet hit the man's shoulder spinning him sideways. "Next?" He said quietly.

Another of the men spoke. Jack shot him in the leg. A lot of hand-gesturing and words in Mandarin, and the four released their prize and limped or ran down the alley, away from their foiled escapade.

Jack helped the young woman to her feet, recovered her shoes, and handed her a loose earring he saw on the ground.

"Thank you for being my guardian angel." She spoke in broken English.

"I need to get to the port," Jack said, "without being seen. Can you help me?"

Chapter Two

Jack Metzger glanced around the small airport as he walked towards the passenger gate. Almost six feet tall with well-defined muscles showing from under his wrinkled t-shirt, he might have been considered good-looking but for his unkempt appearance. His dark brown eyes looked hard and sleep deprived. He wore torn khaki shorts and flip flops, all looking like they needed a good wash. Heading towards the front of the airport, Jack's mind was elsewhere. *God this place is empty. I need to figure out how to get a new identity. I can't continue to be Jack Metzger what with goons breathing down my neck.* So immersed in his own thoughts, he stumbled over the only other passenger's suitcase.

At that moment, the passenger deplaned from the small commuter aircraft and walked towards his now upside-down suitcase.

"Sorry man. I'm a clumsy ox," Jack said to the stranger.

"Not true, totally my fault. This bag is cumbersome and old. It's seen a lot of mileage. It doesn't help I'm toting a box too."

"Let me help you." Jack took the large box from the man.

The man with the salt and peppered head of hair gave Jack a nodding thank you and smiled.

"I should introduce myself. I'm Paul Kanga, new pastor at the Good News Church. Do you have a ride into town? The least I can do is give you a lift." The minister, almost the same height as Jack, wore casual Hawaiian clothes and sandals.

"I'm Jack Metzger and that would be great." Jack studied the man and gave him a friendly grin. "Mahalo, it saves me from getting a taxi or using my thumb on the highway. Don't relish hitchhiking from here to Kaunakakai."

"Happy to do it," said Paul.

As the sun disappeared into an emerald splash on the horizon behind them, the two men walked across the dirt parking lot of the Hoolehua Airport. Paul found an old car with his name on the windshield. With difficulty, he opened the car door, searched on the floor of the front seat and found a key under a frayed floor mat. Feeling an accomplishment, he climbed in and put the key into the ignition.

"My god, an old '39 Packard," Jack exclaimed. "I'm surprised it's still running." He looked at the weather-rusted car as he opened the passenger side door. "We had one of these babies when I was stationed on Molokai during the war." Gingerly, he sat down on the seat's bent, sagging springs.

"You were here during the war?" Paul gave Jack an incredulous look.

"And before the war. You should have seen this place then." Jack told Paul what it was like when he arrived on Molokai. "All the scuttlebutt was about the war and war preparation. It all began in '39 before I arrived. World War II brought many changes to the little town of Kaunakakai. The president asked the commanding general of the U.S. Army to assume the role of military governor. Martial law was enacted when Japan attacked Pearl, an airbase and barracks were formed at the airport where we landed, and the army and navy swelled the numbers of people now residing on Molokai. Concrete bunkers were built every few hundred yards around the shoreline. Food was scarce for the native population. If you weren't growing your own, times were even tougher. No fishing allowed, but people did it anyway, by no light just for food.

"Except for very few Japanese, who had been trusted workers for years, Japanese families were moved off the island to relocation camps. The Hawaiians occupied the homesteads, the Filipinos the Ranch Camp."

"It truly must have been more than an exciting time."

"I suppose so. All I remember is following orders."

Paul laughed.

"The Navy already had its emergency disaster plan in place. The Army would administer and coordinate war related civilian activities in the event of attack. In summer of '41, I took part in a mock battle showing the island's vulnerability. The newspapers all said Japan might strike the islands in November."

"They almost had it right," Paul said.

"I bivouacked here at this very spot. See where

13

those old buildings are at the far end of the runway?"

"Same buildings?"

"Could be. I still think about the way the islanders lived on what they grew. There used to be a country store owned by the Molokai Ranch people. During the war, their store stocked most of the food for the island. Without that store, I doubt many of the islanders would have survived."

Paul listened intently as Jack told him about his experiences on the island. "Since you've been here before, here's the map the church gave me. You can navigate." Paul put an old map into Jack's lap.

"When I left this place in '46, it looked deserted. Over twenty years since I set foot on this soil. Nothing seems changed."

As Paul drove out of the airport, Jack laughed at the sign he saw hanging on a wire fence. *Go Slow It's Molokai.* "See what I mean?" Jack said, pointing out the sign to Paul.

"Did you ever hear the song about Kaunakakai?"

"No, never. Do you mean this place has a song about it?"

"Some celebrity had a song written about him." Jack began to sing the words.

> *He wore a malo and a coconut hat*
> *One for this and the other for that*
> *All the people shouted as he went by*
> *He was the cockeyed mayor of Kaunakakai.*

"It's been so long, I'm surprised I remembered the words."

"Did anyone ever tell you, you have a nice

voice?"

"Not since my Ma. She died a long time ago."

"Where's home for you, Jack?"

"A small town in Oklahoma. My Daddy was the Baptist preacher. Mean to the core, a real son of a bitch. 'Scuse the language, Paul, but that's how I describe him. I left home right after we buried my Ma. Never went back. I didn't want to see that bastard again, too many bad memories."

"Sorry I brought it up, but you do have a nice voice."

Darkness had settled over the island. Without a moon, and on the deserted road to town, Jack's mind raced. He thought about the island topography.

Jack's thoughts were turning in a darker direction. *Can I steal Paul's identity? The highway is pretty damn deserted. I'd hate to kill him, but I need his papers. I guess I don't have much choice. I wonder where he keeps his wallet? Right pocket? Left pocket?*

Jack looked out the window at the highway. He thought he saw a turnout ahead. "Paul, I need to take a leak. Would you find a good place to stop the car?"

Paul did as Jack asked when he spotted the hard dirt on the side of the highway. Jack exited the Packard and walked toward the cliff. He relieved himself, walked a few more steps, and called to Paul. "Paul, you've got to see this."

Paul left the car and walked towards Jack. Jack began to remove a knife hidden in his waistband, but thought better of it when he heard Paul call out. "Jack, help me." Paul staggered towards Jack and keeled over onto the ground.

By the time Jack reached Paul, he realized the mark he had chosen was dead. Stunned, at first Jack didn't move. "Must have had a heart attack. Too bad, you were a hell of a nice guy, Paul, but I need your identity and I'm going to take it. At least you won't need it anymore." With military precision, Jack removed Paul's sports jacket being careful it wouldn't acquire grass stains. *This is a nice jacket and I think it will fit me.* He checked Paul's pants pockets, found four ten-dollar bills, a couple of ones, and identification. Jack quickly shoved all the items into his own shorts pocket before dragging Paul's body to the edge of the cliff. He shoved the corpse over the cliff into the roaring surf below. *If I remember right, there shouldn't be any traces of Paul's body. The sharks will make quick work of it when they find him.*

Glad he didn't have to kill Paul but feeling ill at ease from taking his money and identification, Jack drove at a slow pace along the highway looking for the church. *At least it'll be a roof over my head until I can move on. Paul told me no one from the church had met him. There's no goons chasing me, and thankfully, I avoided Charlene when I left. She's a great lay but a lot more trouble.* Jack continued down the carless road until he saw a tiny green and white church. Its white sign in black lettering said it was the Church of Good News. He steered the rusted Packard into a dirt driveway and stopped under a covered space. Now the sky was pitch black, but he saw a side door and hoped it led to the rectory where the minister would reside. He remembered how lax Kaunakakai residents were about locking doors. Finding the door unlocked, Jack walked through it. Once he found the light switch, he went back to the car trunk, and pulled out the large suitcase and the box he had carried for Paul. He locked himself inside the house and carried the suitcase into the safety of the rectory bedroom. *Don't need any strangers looking for me just yet.*

Jack sat on the bed beside the case he opened and pulled out a sheaf of papers. He found a letter inviting Paul Kanga to be the new minister of the small church. Feeling relief after arriving safely inside the church doors, Jack stretched his arms and scrunched them behind his back. He felt gratitude towards Paul for giving him a new identity, but realized he should have left his Jack Metzger identification on him. *I know I'll be okay. Goons wouldn't be looking for a pastor.*

"Shit," he said aloud. "Ministers preach." He then continued muttering to himself. "What can I remember from my father's sermons? I know I can be a lot kinder than he was. I know I can do this. The church sign outside says service is at ten on Sunday. I'll have a few days to prepare something. If I don't preach, I can't masquerade as a minister. Jeez, how many sermons will I have to give before I can get away from this god forsaken place? Hell, Jack, you've been in tough places before. Get a grip."

Jack felt his stomach rumble. *Wonder if there's any food in the house?* He traveled to the kitchen to discover some kind souls from the church had fully stocked the pantry with canned goods. *This must be my lucky day.*

Believing a minister would keep his house neat, Jack emptied the suitcase on the bed, hung up all the clothes from it in the closet, folded the underwear and socks, and put them in a dresser drawer. He looked at the shoes and sandals he had tossed on the floor and realized he and Paul wore the same size. *It's strange I didn't see that before.* Needing to get rid of his dirty clothes, Jack found an old aloha shirt and some dark shorts, he undressed and hopped into the shower. He soaped his hair and body, staying under the shower head until he no longer saw soap bubbles. Once he had dried himself off, he removed the bedspread and turned down the sheet. *Now I want to sleep. When I wake up, Jack Metzger will cease to exist.* He looked at the brown box. *I'll look inside that box tomorrow.* Jack crashed on the bed and fell into a deep sleep.

Early 1930s, somewhere in Oklahoma

The young boy knelt on a grainy salt patch his father poured on the floor. His skinny body was bare except for underpants, grayed with age.

"Don't you move, Jack. You can't get up until you can recite the entire Psalm I'm using in my Sunday sermon." The man stood over him with his leather belt ready for use at any moment. Jack's back showed angry red welts as proof of what his father could do.

The boy tried to be stoic, but water clouded his eyes. The salt dug into his kneecaps, and he knew they had begun bleeding.

"Jack, you're a miserable excuse for a son. I asked you to chop some wood and bring it in for the stove."

"But I did, Daddy. I did 'xactly as you asked."

"Don't sass me, young whippersnapper. I'll take my belt to you again."

Molokai, 1960s

Jack awakened with a start. *Another nightmare to end all nightmares. Will they ever stop? Yet I feel safe in my new skin and my new name.* He talked to himself. "I haven't thought about him since I ran away. He was the meanest son of a bitch anyone could have for a father. How could he have been a minister? He slapped around Ma, until she was too weak to resist and died from overwork. If I must be a minister to escape being killed by the cartel, I'll do it. Further, I'll never be unkind to anyone. I never wanted to dispose of Paul's body, but survival was the only thing on my mind. I got myself in pretty deep when that drug shipment was stolen. I don't ever want anything to do with drugs, or the people I dealt with in Singapore."

Jack sat up and raised his arm with a fist. "God, I will do whatever is in my power to stay alive. I swear."

The next day the new Paul dressed in the minister's clothes, slid into the sandals he found, gave his hair a cursory hand-comb, and decided his first errand of the day would be to find a barber.

As he drove off to town, down the only highway, he realized 'his' church was one of many lining one side of the road. He saw a barbershop on the main drag and pulled the car into an empty parking spot. Ala Malama was a dusty, semi-paved road, and the humid hot weather did nothing to soothe his anxiety.

"Got time to give me a haircut?" he asked the barber.

"Sit right down, brudda. Are you new in town?"

"I'm Paul Kanga, the new minister at the Good News Church. Haven't had a decent haircut in weeks. Glad you had free time." Jack smiled at him.

They chit-chatted banalities while the barber cut his hair.

"Where you from?" asked the barber.

"Palau was where I had my last church," Jack replied. "Got a calling to Kaunakakai. I'm looking forward to a long and happy association. For me, this is wonderful civilization when compared to my last church. I'm truly looking forward to preaching here."

"We got a lot of churches here. I ain't never been to that one. Wish you success, Pastor."

"By any chance do you know a Joe Obregon? We were in the service together. I thought he might have come back to Molokai. Lost track of him several years ago."

"Pastor, he's one bad dude, and spends most time being drunk. I wouldn't go into any bar looking for him. Always drunk and huhu, you're likely to find your jaw at the end of his fist. You might find him on his boat. He ties up at the pier."

"Thanks for the warning and the information." *Joe, you always managed to find trouble. Why in the hell did you get me back here? This will be the last time I'll come find you. I've got bigger fish to fry. I'm heading for Hong Kong and Macao as soon as I can get away from this god-forsaken place.*

"Obregon," the barber said, "went lolo when he found out his ex-wife had married his former best friend. She's a wonderful woman, a teacher, with three smart kids. One son is a school principal here in Kaunakakai, just like his stepfather. Another is our doctor on the island. And the daughter, I'm not sure what she does."

Jack took in everything the barber told him. *Best to be forewarned. I hope they never learn my real identity. I didn't kill Paul, but I did get rid of the body. I'll have to stay long enough to leave without suspicion. Now that I look presentable, I'll let people know I'm looking for Joe. Like the barber said, I'm sure he's in some bar, but I don't think I'll have to check it out. Ministers don't go inside those dens of iniquity.* He chuckled to himself.

Chapter Three

Two young boys were fishing off the side of the town wharf when one of them spied something floating on the rocks beneath the end of the pier.

"It looks like a funny kind a fish."

"That's a body, Danh," the older boy, Akoni, said. "I've got to run to the police station and report it. You stay here." His voice sounded authoritative to his younger brother.

"I'm not staying with no dead body," Danh said, grabbing Akoni's arm. "I'm going with you."

The two of them stashed their fishing equipment against the side of a shed and ran the short distance to the police station. Inside the front door, they were met by a hefty policeman who towered over them.

"Mr. Policeman, we found a dead body in the water," the boys said in chorus.

"Are you playing a joke on me, boys?" George

Kapule smiled at them.

"No, sir, come with us, you'll see," said Akoni.

George looked at them. "All right, boys, we'll take my car." The boys were put in the back seat. The doors locked behind them. They looked at each other, their faces grim.

George drove to the wharf and opened the door for the boys. "Where did you see this body?"

"On the rocks, under the pier," said Akoni. The excitement in his voice mounted.

The boys had to run to keep up with the officer's stride.

"See there." Akoni pointed to the bloated remains of the man floating face down in the water.

After seeing the body for himself, the officer radioed for an ambulance to take the body to the clinic where there was some semblance of a mortuary. He affixed yellow tape around the entire area and radioed again for another police car.

"Get Junior over here," he said over the radio. "We have a mystery on our hands. From what I can see, the deceased has no visible wounds. But why would the body end up in the ocean? The corpse is pretty damn bloated, must have floated into the pilings, but so big, it couldn't go back to the ocean without a strong outgoing tide. The coroner can tell us a lot more details once the body is examined. I'm surprised the sharks didn't get him."

"Can you identify the guy?" the voice on the other end of the line asked.

"The face looks familiar, but I don't know him. When a body is bloated, the facial features change. He's not Hawaiian, but not haole either. Right now, he's just a John Doe, nothing in his pockets to identify him. I don't see any shark marks on him either. Amazing to me."

George, the most senior member of the Molokai police force, then took the boys back to the station so he could question them further.

"Who's your Dad, Akoni?"

"Mikala Palani, you must know him. He's the high school principal."

"And your grandmother is Malia Palani?"

"Yes."

"You have a very nice grandmother. She taught me in school."

The boys began to relax a little when they realized the policeman was just trying to be friendly with them. There didn't seem to be much more they could tell him.

"Boys, if I need to ask you any more questions, I know where to find you. I'll just come out to the house. Is that okay with you?"

The boys nodded their assent. George sat down at his desk after the boys left, thinking this man had to have arrived on the island recently. He decided to call the airline and get a manifest from the plane that landed a couple of days previously.

"Two people disembarked," said the person on the other end of the line. "One was a minister. I heard him say the words 'good news' in their conversation."

"Thanks," said George and put down the receiver.

He decided to pay a visit to the new minister at Good News Church.

Jack answered the door. Upon seeing the officer, he gave him a large smile. "I'm Pastor Paul Kanga, the new minister of this church. How can I help you?".

"I'm George Kapule, Chief of Police. This is not the best way to introduce myself but I have a dead body on my hands."

"You must have a lot on your mind. How did the man die?" Paul looked concerned. "I haven't really even settled in. The only thing I've done is get a haircut. I looked pretty scruffy on arrival." *I'm getting pretty damn glib at telling tales. Just have to keep my stories straight.* "Can I invite you in for a cup of coffee? Not the best cook, but the coffee is good."

"I didn't say anything to the boys who discovered the body, but I think the man they found in the water might be someone who lived here before the war. Obregon was his last name."

Jack nodded. Surprised to hear the name Obregon, he didn't want to acknowledge to the police he had come to Molokai to find him. "I only arrived a couple of days ago. I'm preaching my first sermon this Sunday. About the only people I've had contact with at the church has been by phone. I'm not familiar with anyone who worships in this congregation. I met the town barber. I was stationed here during World War II and for about a year in '46. From what I can see, the only change has been the size of the trees in the grove across the highway. They've grown quite a bit in the last twenty years."

George laughed and nodded. "My guess is you didn't meet many of the civilian population while you were here. Obregon deserted his family in San Diego right after the war," he said. "Malia, his wife, returned to Molokai with three babies, raised them while attending school and studying to be a teacher at the same time. Mike Palani Senior was one of Obregon's best friends before the war. They canoed together, and competed against each other all the time. Track, football, baseball—it didn't matter. When Malia came back, Mike pursued her and married her. Obregon showed up on Ala Malama about six months ago, trying to find her, and said he wanted her back. Big brouhaha, especially when he found out she was happily married to Mike. We all think he's gone a little crazy, since so much time had elapsed from when they were still married. The kids are all grown and doing well. Those little boys who found the body would have been Obregon's grandchildren."

George asked Jack a few more questions.

"I think that's all the information I'm going to need for now. I need to get back the end of the pier and make certain the area stays closed off as a crime scene. What a terrible thing to happen. If it's a murder, it will be the first murder on Molokai."

"Murder is bad anytime."

"I know, but the weekend after next we are having a special celebration at the cultural center. Malia Palani is in charge of all the activities, and she's been working for over a year putting it all together. We're also having a big luau. Lots of talk story and music. It would be a shame to see it spoiled by a mysterious death. You're planning on coming, aren't you?"

"I didn't know about any festivities on the island. Saturdays, I usually spend finishing my Sunday sermon, but I'll be glad to put in an appearance."

"Good. Kaunakakai is one big ohana, and it would be a great way for a newcomer to meet a lot of its residents. I know Malia's family doesn't attend your church, but it would be nice for you to meet them since part of her family are your neighbors."

"Do you have any more questions for me?"

"Not at this time, Pastor, but I do appreciate any help you might have, especially if you can remember seeing or hearing anything from your arrival at the airport."

"I will. Nice to have met you, officer." Jack walked George to the rectory doorway. *What if the police discover I knew Joe Obregon from his tour of duty in the Navy. I'll have to be careful to keep my story straight.*

"Same here pastor, mahalo."

Well if it is Joe, I don't have anything to worry about, but I'm sure it's the man who died, and whose identity I stole. His mind conjured up all kinds of scenarios. *How in the hell did his body wind up at the wharf? When I threw him off the cliff, I thought for sure he would be shark bait. I've got all his papers though showing I'm Pastor Paul Kanga. Maybe I should have left Jack Metzger's wallet in his pants pocket. It's too late to worry about that now. I'll take a look in that box tonight.*

Chapter Four

Malia could be heard singing in the kitchen while she prepared dinner for her family. Her body ached from all the lifting and sorting of quilts for her show. She knew she was tired, working without stop for several months collecting quilts from the old aunties and their families. The last few weeks she had worked from early morning to almost sunset preparing for the quilt show. People would be coming from all over the island, and even flying in for this Hawaiian celebration.

The opening of Kalanianaole Hall, the new cultural center would be on Saturday, and Malia organized the quilt show to coincide with the center's opening. Kaunakakai had been buzzing with all the preparations. The first of its kind in the islands, the quilt show was expected to draw visitors from everywhere. Molokai's population had never seen such excitement. Malia's entire family, including her grandchildren, would be there.

Malia looked out to enjoy the scenery beyond the lanai of the home she and Mike had built together. The house overlooked the Pacific from almost every room, and Malia never tired watching the turquoise sea with its ever-changing colors. Her thoughts returned her to childhood when she began making quilts, first taught by her great-grandmother and then her mother. Her reverie wandered to those early days of running through the fields barefoot, finding trees with lovely smelling plumeria. She remembered falling asleep amidst a sea of blossoms that had fallen on the warm dirt...

... Cutting fabric was a very monotonous task. She saw herself cut, cut, cut...

"Mom, Mom, are you all right?" Her daughter Leilani turned the water faucet off.

"Oh, Leilani, I must have been day dreaming."

"Yes, and you almost caused a flood in the kitchen." A pretty girl with a slender build and shiny black hair, Leilani laughed as she hugged her mother.

"Honey, you can help me prepare dinner since you're here," said Malia. Malia stood just a shade under Leilani's height. Her raven-colored hair showed only a few strands of gray. Malia braided it and wore it on top of her head in a crown. The regal manner of her hair style had nothing to do with Malia's sweet personality. "Could you please pick some tomatoes and lettuce from the garden? There's a pineapple for a fruit salad. You can add some papaya and mango, too. Thanks, my darling." Malia, an older version of her daughter, pushed back black hair strands falling into her face and smiled. *I'm so lucky to have such a beautiful daughter.*

"Mom, I have some news from town. I didn't want to even tell you on the phone."

Malia went to the refrigerator and took out a pitcher of iced tea.

"Well, let me pour us each a glass of tea, and we can sit down, and you can tell me the latest."

"Mikala's boys found a dead body in the rocks at the end of the pier." Leilani wasted no time with her shocking revelation.

"Good lord, those poor tykes. Did the police identify the body? Did you learn anything else?" Malia set down her glass, aghast at the news.

"George Kapule labeled the body as a John Doe. He'd never seen the person before, although he looked familiar. George didn't tell me anything more, but I heard the man had no visible markings on him, like a bullet hole or a stab wound."

"I hope they find out who the man is. But if it wasn't murder, who put his body into the ocean and why?"

"Knowing George, he'll be a bloodhound until he finds the person who did it."

The two of them sat on the lanai drinking their tea. Leilani picked up a quilt she hadn't seen before. "Mom, is this one going in the show?"

Malia nodded as she swallowed a small gulp of tea.

"It has a date sewed on it. You must have been about fourteen when you quilted this one."

"My ulu quilt. Couldn't believe someone returned it to me at the house a couple of days ago. I wonder where they found it."

Malia's eyes took on a faraway look as she studied the date, 1935. "So many important things happened in those years. I had a brother Richard who was recruited to colonize Howland Island. We never saw him again, except in snapshots. He was killed at the beginning of the war."

"How terrible, Mom. I didn't know the family lost anyone during the war. You've never talked about him. Grandma and Grandpa must have been devastated when he died."

"They were. But for me, it was also the year I met Joao Obregon."

"At that time, it must have been good. How strange life treats us." Leilani's words sounded philosophical.

Malia's mind drifted back in time.

I try so hard to forget this period in my life. How different my life might have been if that treacherous storm hadn't stranded a schooner and the strangers on board hadn't rowed to the nearest island where they saw signs of life. When did that happen? Although so long ago it seems like yesterday...

Molokai, 1935

... The sand filtered through Malia's toes as she waded near the shore. The warm water lapped softly over her feet. She loved to come to the beach at Coconut Grove to watch the honu. There the sea turtles basked in all their glory, their shells nice and shiny. The turtles paddled around as their heads bobbed up out of the water every so often. Malia ran her fingers through her long shiny black hair. Using her hand, she shaded her eyes from the sun. Today, Malia was more interested in what was happening out beyond the reef. She watched an old sailing ship as it limped along in the channel between Molokai and Lanai. It was too far away for her to see clearly, but now, it looked like whoever was on board was trying to set the anchors. Soon after, she noticed men rowing a boat towards the harbor.

"Malahinis," she exclaimed. Malia realized what excitement the newcomers would bring to everyone. She ran home as fast as her legs could carry her. Even though it was 1935, the island of Molokai was considered the far ends of the earth. Mainly known because of Father Damien and the leper colony, it was not a place where tourists readily visited. Whether by marriage, hanai, or blood, most of the island inhabitants were related to each other. The island was a friendly place where many people still followed the old Hawaiian traditions.

Malia walked with her father, Akane, and mother, Noelani, and several other locals to the harbor. They carried leis they had made to welcome the newcomers. As Malia and the other women and girls greeted them, a lei was placed over the head of each sailor as he approached.

The captain spoke a little English and managed to communicate the identity of the landing party and where they were from. A monstrous storm had devastated their sails, the mast was broken. There was other damage to the schooner as well, which stranded them in the high seas before they could reach their planned destination of Honolulu.

This ill-fated voyage had been Joao Obregon's first trip to the sea. He had signed on to serve as crew on a pleasure yacht. Only part of the crew and the captain were still on board, the others were lost at sea. Joao's trip was only supposed to last for one year, but they were well into their second. Extensive storm damage caused the limping of the boat into the harbor. Now Joao knew it would be almost two years before he would arrive back in Portugal.

Joao officially met Malia when Akane invited the captain and all the men from the ship to join him and his family at a luau. After some passengers drowned and the boat was demolished by the raging storm, this would be a celebration of the survivors' safe arrival. Joao sat next to Malia at the luau.

"Take the coconut like this." She used a mallet to crack the shell. She demonstrated how to drink from the coconut.

"Now, you can drink the milk inside. You try it now."

Joao smiled and nodded his head. A handsome young man, with his black hair, dark eyes and well-tanned skin, he could have been mistaken for a native.

When they met, Joao couldn't speak a word of English, but he fell under the spell of Malia, and thought she was one of the most beautiful girls he had ever seen. Every day when he was finished with his duties for the captain, he would search her out. She taught him English, one word at a time. A quick learner, he managed to speak more than a few sentences in a short span of time.

Joao, a handsome young man with well-developed muscles for a teenager, followed Malia around town like a shy puppy dog. She was glad for the stranger's company. He seemed so nice. Malia introduced him to all her friends, but especially Mike Palani. They hit it off at once. Mike introduced Joao to canoeing. Once Joao knew more English, Mike also told him about our special time on the island with the Makahiki games. Joao thought it sounded like great sport, parading with all the banners, the dancing and hand-to-hand combat.

He loved hearing the stories about the Hawaiian gods and how the games came into being. Being Catholic, however, he wasn't certain how to assimilate this information into his own religion. "In Hawaiian lore, God is in three parts," explained Malia. "Kane the creator; Lono, the sustainer of life; and Kanaloa, the gift of death. The Makahiki games pay homage to Lono, the god of agriculture. The various tribes or athletic groups, sometimes schools, prepare distinctive tribal banners with decorative designs, all in one color representing their group. They bring offerings to Lono before the games competition. They bring gifts of fresh spring water, sweet potatoes, ti plants and other crops his followers believe he will like. Crowns of ti leaves and leis of the same are the only adornments of the muscular men in white muslin loin cloths, except for the tattoos on their bodies. A parade with all the participants and their banners is a beautiful sight. There is hula dancing. All the kapunas or elderly are revered at this ceremony. They are escorted to special seats. A horn is heard, and the games begin. They test the skill, and agility of all the participants. Makahiki is a Molokai tradition, so groups come from the other islands to participate. Even though we all go to the church of our choosing, there is still a reverence to Lono. It's taken very seriously by all of us who are Hawaiians. The games may be a lot of fun, but it is an important ceremony. The gifts to Lono are to ensure fresh water and good health, just to name two."

"Can I participate?" Joao asked.

"If you're still here," Mike said.

"Well, when the captain and his ship are ready

to leave, I'll be sailing with them. But I plan to be back. You can count on it."

Malia ran her hand through her long black hair waiting to say something. "Hula dancing is what you saw today, and it originated here on Molokai."

"It looks like it might be fun, but isn't it hard to learn?" Joao asked.

"I'll teach you." Malia smiled.

"I'm counting on that."

"I'm counting on it, too," she thought.

Molokai, 1950s

… "Mom, are you counting how many quilts will be on display?"

"What, what? Oh, Leilani, I must really be tired. What did you ask me?"

"Have you counted how many quilts we're displaying?"

"There's about thirty in the entire show. This particular one was made when I returned with you and Kimo and Mikala to the islands."

"All of a sudden you looked so sad."

"I was just remembering all that had happened when I made this quilt."

"Mom, please tell me about it. You never talk about our birth father. I've been told he is back on Molokai."

"Well, thankfully, I haven't seen him. I wouldn't know what to say or do. I haven't seen him since 1947. He broke my heart. My wonderful dear Mike put it back together again. It's almost a lifetime ago. You were just a baby. I don't talk about Joe because of the terrible things he did to me and your brothers. Your stepfather, Mike, has truly been your real father."

"I'd like to know more about Joe and the quilt, if it's not too difficult. It looks like tear drops. You must have been very sad when you made it."

"You're absolutely right, darling. They represent my tears. Making the quilt helped me stop crying and feeling sorry for myself. I had the three of you to care for and not much money to do it. I went back to school so I could teach on the island. I worked as a secretary until I finished. Your father wanted a divorce. He left all of us stranded in San Diego."

"How awful. That's unthinkable."

"Yes, it was, my darling. One night, Joe—that was how he wanted to be called now—became angry at the dinner table for no apparent reason. He told me he had some business to clear up, and after dinner, he rose from the table, put his Navy jacket back on, and walked out the door without saying goodbye to any of us. He never returned."

"As two days turned into three, I became so distraught. I didn't know what to do or where to turn. I remember going to my secretarial teacher. I told her what had happened and she took me to the commander's office. 'Joe's boss man,' she called him. I didn't know. After telling him my story, the boss man sent me to the admiral who was in charge of the base. He told me to sit down in a chair. I tried to be very brave and not cry, but it was hard. I told him what Joe had done, and that he never came home. I also showed him some papers that arrived in the mail. I didn't understand what they said."

"The admiral told me Joe had reenlisted the week before, and requested overseas duty. He was already on his way to his new assignment, in a place called the Mediterranean. The admiral showed me where it was on a map. That was my first geography lesson."

"Oh, my poor sweet mother." Leilani gave her a big hug and kiss, wiping away her few tears. "I'm sorry I interrupted you. But I want to hear more."

Malia reached for a handkerchief from a pocket in her dress, blew her nose, and continued. "Then the admiral told me the papers said since Joe and I weren't married in the Catholic Church, Joe didn't feel we were really married. He had no desire to continue the marriage. The admiral said Joe felt no responsibility towards me or you kids. The admiral also informed me I would have to go to court. When I did, the judge would see to it I received money each month for all of us.

"I was bereft. My tears flowed as if a dam had burst. Why had Joe done this? Besides being huhu all the time, I thought he went lolo. He had no reason to be angry with me. I didn't understand why he didn't love me anymore. How could he leave the four of us? You were a baby, Leilani. I couldn't believe the cruelty of his words. To say we weren't married. I couldn't believe he had changed so much."

Leilani could see her mother was visibly upset from their conversation. She got up from her chair, put her arms around her mother, and again began hugging her and kissing her face. "Our Dad is Mike, Mom, and I will never think of him as anything else. He is so wonderful and so kind."

"Yes, I know, Leilani, and I feel blessed to have him as my husband. I've known him all my life. Your brother Mikala was even named after him."

"But you must have loved Joe at one time,

didn't you?"

"I did. And so did everyone else in Kaunaka-kai. I was only fourteen when we met. I taught him English. I never liked school, so he was helping me to read and write it. Joe was a much quicker learner ...

Molokai, 1935

"Joao, I hate school. Why can't we go and sit on the beach?"

"You must learn, ipo, otherwise your father won't let me marry you. He said you have to graduate high school first. Malia, my ship is returning to Portugal very soon. But I will write you. And I will be back, and we will get married."

"Are you certain, Joao? I will miss you so terribly."

"I will miss you, too. But when I return we will have a beautiful wedding day, and luau..."

Molokai, 1950s

Malia's mind returned to the present, and she continued her story.

"True to his word, Joe wrote me letters. And I answered them. But I had to take them to the priest at St. Sophia's to help me read them. It made me study all the harder so I could read better, and not have to go to the priest seeking help with my letter reading and writing."

"I began making a magnificent white wedding quilt, with small touches of yellow and green. It had honu for the design motif because Joe and I spent so much time watching the turtles. My friends began to question me as to why I was making this quilt when

Joe probably wouldn't return. I kept my faith and kept on working. I found white dress fabric in a Sears catalog and sent for several yards. I knew I didn't want a veil—just a crown of flowers woven into my long, shiny black hair."

Malia continued her story. "Two years passed and Joe still hadn't returned to the island. I had one more year of high school and I would graduate. Your grandparents would look at me and smile, and when I wasn't around shake their heads hoping I wouldn't be hurt too badly when Joe never returned.

"Three weeks after I graduated, the inter-island boat arrived from Honolulu. On board was a young man who couldn't wait to get off. He had his duffel bag over his shoulder, and began trudging up the road toward my home. I saw this figure walking up our road towards the family kuleana, and when I realized it was Joe, I ran to him with open arms. We couldn't hug enough, and neither of us could get a word in edge wise, there was so much to say. 'You came back.' I told him.

"'Of course I did. I love you. When can we get married?' Joe said over and over again.

"I was in seventh heaven. I wanted a true Hawaiian wedding held in the Coconut Grove. The minister from the Episcopal Church officiated. Almost the entire population of Kaunakakai was there to witness the nuptials. The luau was huge, with two roast pigs. Mike and your Uncle Oke, my younger brother, dug the pits and prepared everything for the barbecuing of them. Mike was also best man."

"Uncle Oke, Mike, and a couple other of the bruddas had built us this little hale where we lived with such contentment. We picked plumeria and orchids and made leis to sell at the farmer's market. We picked the mangos and the pineapples and sold them, too. Joe got a job in the pineapple fields, and saved enough money to buy a small fishing boat. He would go out and catch akule, and we would sell most of the fish on Ala Malama, and the rest we ate in the family.

"When I found out I was pregnant, we were beside ourselves with joy. I enjoyed a happy pregnancy until the Japanese bombed Pearl Harbor. We didn't know what was going to happen next. We would be glued to the radio, afraid we might miss an important message. The soldiers made us put black curtains over the windows at night.

"It was scary. Military personnel already were here on the island, but more came and built these huge concrete bunkers every six hundred feet or so. They took over the airport and built barracks. We lived under martial law. All civilians had a curfew unless they were exempt because of their job. Joe and I talked about what we would do, and the next thing I knew, Joe told me he and Mike and Kimo Pascua were going to take a canoe, and paddle to Honolulu to see what they could do for the war effort."

"I said, 'Joao I'm going to have our baby.' He said, 'Ipo, sweetheart, we want to talk to the Navy and see what we can do to help.'

"'I'm frightened. How can I get along without you?' I asked.

"He said, 'You'll be just fine. Your mother will help you. Molokai has a hospital, and I'm told the island has a good midwife. Our baby will be healthy. He is an Obregon.'"

Malia moved from the punai to the flowered couch, made herself comfortable, and continued her story. "I had been working on a keiki quilt for the new baby, but when Joe told me of his plans, I was beside myself. After he left for Honolulu, I sat in our hale and rarely went outside. My parents tried to bring me out of my shell, but I was inconsolable. One of mother's friends brought me some new fabric, bright red and blue."

"Is that one of the quilts I still have to hang?" asked Leilani.

"Yes, that quilt showed my pain. I cut the material into small shreds, and little by little, I would sew each shred onto my sheet backing. It was difficult, painstaking work, but the quilt began to take shape. The red represented bloodshed of our troops, the white for the innocence of our country, and the blue for loyalty."

"Mom, it's absolutely beautiful. I'm certain it will be the hit of the show."

"I can't believe the show starts next Saturday. Do you think we're ready?"

"Of course we are, Mom. You're fantastic. Now, will you please tell me the rest of the story?" Leilani prodded her mother to continue.

"When I received the divorce papers sent by your birth father, it left me reeling. We were all still in San Diego. I'm still grateful we weren't across the country. San Diego was far enough. With the Navy's assistance, aided by a local social service agency, I packed all our personal belongings, all our clothes, and every toy. The admiral who was in charge of the naval base found a ship sailing to Honolulu from Long Beach harbor, so he secured us passage. The social service lady put me and the three of you on a Greyhound bus to Los Angeles. At the station, we were met by another social service lady who saw that we were transferred to another bus that took us to the harbor."

"With three small children, that sounds like a feat in itself to transport all of us."

"You were all amazingly good. I was so proud of you."

"What happened next?"

"The boys were wide-eyed when they saw the ship that would take us to Honolulu. You just wanted to be held. I wouldn't let any of you outside the cabin unless I was with you. Otherwise, we stayed inside the cabin, played games, and I had to figure out ways to entertain you all. The ship took ten days before it arrived in Honolulu. When we did arrive, someone helped us aboard an inter-island freighter. That took us several long hours before we arrived at the Kaunakakai Wharf."

"I don't remember any of this."

"You were too small darling."

"Did grandfather come to meet us?"

"No, no one was there when we disembarked at the pier. They didn't know we were coming. I realized neither the boys nor I could manage our belongings because the luggage weighed more than I did. I set everything down next to a small shed on the pier."

"But, Mom, that pier is nowhere near where we live."

"I know, darling. It was actually a several-mile walk to where we needed to go. You were exhausted, and wanted to be carried. Each of your brothers took turns carrying you so I wouldn't have to do it all myself. My little hale was still standing, and no one was living in it. I put you down on the front steps and asked your brothers to watch you. I didn't even look inside before I walked another half mile to where your grandparents had their small farm."

"Mom, you must have been ready to drop. Three kids, luggage. Oh, my gosh."

"I was but I was so happy to be in warm loving arms. I reveled in the inviting welcome of my family. Your Uncle Oke immediately took me in the old pick-up to bring all of you and our luggage back to your grandparents. My parents hadn't even seen you before this. Your brothers barely remembered anyone. Their eyes lit up when they started meeting all their cousins.

"'Almost enough for a football team,' Uncle Oke exclaimed.

"I was so happy to be surrounded by my oha-na. I knew my face lit up, and I smiled for the first time in many months."

"It's no wonder Akoni doesn't want to be called Joe anymore. I wouldn't either if I were him. What Joe did to all of us was more than terrible."

Malia's face showed a sad smile.

"Yes, it was, but I was content knowing that all of you would be raised just like I was. So really even though the tears were first tears of my unhappiness, they then became my tears of joy." She paused and looked out the window.

"Here comes your father. Do you want to join us for dinner?"

"When I can have your home cooking, Mom, how can I refuse? The smells are so ono."

"Mahalo. Since you're staying, I'll let you set the table too. Let's eat in the lanai. It's going to be a beautiful sunset."

Chapter Five

The old Packard rumbled down the beach road. Jack looked out at the wooden bridge. *That piece of wood isn't worth shit. Probably the same wood since before the war.*

He parked the rusting car under a shade tree, stepped out onto the hard sand, walked a few paces, and crossed the wooden bridge leading to the pier. Several old boats were moored off the pier. He walked out to the end of the docking area and looked to see if he could find Joe Obregon's boat. The worst piece of junk should be it. *Ah yes, there it is, Joe's Folly, aptly named. I wonder if he ever does go fishing.*

"Ahoy, Joe."

"Who the hell wants me?" A very slurred voice pierced the darkness.

"Don't tell me I came all the way from Singapore, and you're not happy to see me."

"Jack, you old bastard. Come on aboard, and grab a beer."

Jack climbed over the gunwale and sat next to Joe.

"My name is now Paul Kanga, and I'm the new minister at the Good News Church."

"What the hell?"

"Needed a new identity. Left Singapore under, shall we say, difficult circumstances."

"How did you invent that name?"

"I didn't. It was in the papers of the man whose identity I took."

"Won't he come looking for you?"

"No, I don't think so. The sharks should have made quite a meal."

"Did you kill him? I know you're damn good with a knife."

"No, he had a massive heart attack, I think. Keeled over on the ground right in front of me."

"Lucky break for you as the police chief is a real bird dog." Changing the subject, he looked Jack directly in the eye. "But how can you be a minister?"

"My father was one." Jack laughed. "I'll manage until I can get off the island again. Enough small talk. What was so important for me to come to Molokai?"

"I want help getting my wife back. She's married to someone else, Mike Palani."

"Joe, you walked out on her, left her and the kids in San Diego twenty years ago. What makes you think you can marry Malia again? Or that she will want to marry you?"

"I'll show her I've changed. I need you to get rid of him."

"I'm confused. Wasn't he your best friend? You were always talking about Mike and you did this or that. How do you expect me to have him vanish?"

"I didn't say vanish. I want him out of the picture. Dead if necessary." Joe cocked his head. "I'm thinking—if you're a minister, I could start attending your church. That way we could keep in contact with each other easily. It would look funny if you walked into a bar or started talking to me on the street. And you can't be on board my boat without being seen. That's a difficult thing to do on an island as small as this."

"That sounds quite plausible. Next Saturday, George Kapule told me there will be a large Hawaiian celebration at the cultural center. Malia has done most of the work, and according to George, it's going to be spectacular."

"How in the hell do you know Kapule? I can't count the number of times he's thrown me in jail."

"He's the policeman I met. He interviewed me about the body found in the rock pilings at this wharf. But let's get back on track. Why don't you go, sober, cleaned up, with no kind of animosity towards anyone. You can say hello to Malia, tell her how wonderful it is to see her, say hello to Mike, perhaps even meet your children—that is if they want to meet you. It would be something very hard to do, but then the public will see an entirely different side to you. I can bump into you inside the door, and in front of everyone, invite you to my church."

Joe looked at Jack and laughed. "It will take me days to sober up. But I'll do it, old buddy. Think it's a great idea. I can even tell them we met on a ship going to the Med."

It was almost midnight by the time Jack returned to the church rectory. He had to write his sermon. He also wanted time to go through Paul Kanga's belongings. *I should never have dumped Paul's body. I should have just exchanged identification. What I did is already on my conscience. I don't want or need any more. I'll figure out some way to dissuade him. Joe should be in church on Sunday. I'll give a sermon about Jeremiah. Won't Joe be surprised.*

"And so, brothers and sisters, Jeremiah, a very human prophet, holds up the world as a mirror. He makes it clear to us we are chosen by God. You are chosen. And what makes us holy is doing right and just in the land. God bless you all. Let us pray.

"Almighty God and Father, give us your wisdom as we share our concerns, dreams and prayers in Jesus' name. Come Holy Spirit. Amen."

After services, the pastor stood by the door greeting everyone and shaking their hands.

"If I hadn't seen your name on the church sign, I would never have entered the door. Paul Kanga, are you really a minister now?"

"Joe Obregon, as I live and breathe, I can't believe you returned to Molokai. I've been pastoring ever since I left the Navy over ten years ago. How are you? What are you doing here? I thought you never wanted to see the islands again. Do we have time for a meal, Joe?" Paul Kanga peppered Joe with questions and comments, making certain anyone who hadn't planned to be at the quilt exhibit would know he and Joe knew each other from the Navy.

"Hope you have food to cook, as everything is closed on Sundays."

"I'll figure out something, even if it's spam and eggs."

The last of the congregation departed, having

heard the exchange between Joe and Jack. Joe, whom they saw most times as inebriated and mean, was stone-cold sober. People were shaking their heads in disbelief. But if asked, they had seen it up close.

Joe followed Jack into the rectory. Once the door was locked, the two of them sat in the kitchen and laughed.

"That was the show of the century. I know it will be spread around town. You just have to stay sober now, Joe. If you do, I can even go fishing on your boat with you."

"You're asking a lot of me, Jack, I mean Paul. I'll try."

"You've got to be in good shape to run into Malia next Saturday. Half-sober isn't going to cut the mustard."

"I said I'd try."

"Not enough. You want Malia to see you as a changed person, changed for the better."

"I know, I know."

"Hope you like scrambled eggs," said Jack as he dropped the beaten eggs into the hot frying pan.

That night the faux Paul went through Paul Kanga's box. *I'll be damned. There's a stack of sermons here. What's this?* He pulled out a legal document and looked at it. Paul Kanga is acquitted of all charges, but ordered to leave Palau within thirty days. *Wonder what he did to be accused? Was the good pastor already coming here under a cloud? Maybe he wasn't as good a person he was reputed to be. I'll be happy to use his sermons though. I wonder if there is any way to find out what he did to cause the court to order him to leave.*

Chapter Six

Today meant grocery shopping day in the Palani household. Not an exciting task, but Malia had forgone shopping for almost two weeks because of the quilt show. Now that it was over, she wanted to concentrate on her family. *Misaki's for Kalbe ribs and a couple of roast chickens for the weekend. Young Mike and his family, Kimo and a friend, Leilani and who knows? – I love it whenever our big family gets together. Never a dull moment. The little ones will probably want to play football.*

She was deep in thought when she felt a tap on her shoulder.

"Malia, Malia. It's so good to see you."

She looked at the person talking to her. *It couldn't be. But it looks like him.* "Joe? Joe? Is it you?"

"Me in the flesh, baby. You look wonderful. How are you? I went to the quilt show but I was afraid to talk to you with all the people around. I even remembered when you made some of those quilts."

"Yes. I imagine you would."

"Come into the bakery and have a cup of coffee with me."

"I really shouldn't, Joe. I have a lot of errands to run for the family."

"Can't you spare the time for one cup of java?"

"One cup, Joe, that's all, and then I must get back to my errands."

"All right. I'll accept that. I have something important I would like to talk to you about."

Once they both ordered their coffee and brought it to a table in the back, Joe spoke. "Malia, I'm the most stupid man in the world for letting you go, and I apologize for everything I did that was wrong."

Malia was dumbfounded at his words because they sounded sincere, because he looked directly into her eyes. "That was a long time ago, Joe, I've moved on."

"I just want you back, ipo. I want our life like it used to be, happy and uncomplicated."

"You're about twenty years too late for that, Joe. My life is very happy now."

He grabbed her arm hard. "Malia, you're mine. You always have been. You always will be."

Malia pulled away from him and stood up from the table.

"Joe, please. Don't speak to me like that, or try to contact me again. You'll only make things worse—more difficult for you." Malia was adamant. She felt fearful from Joe's actions.

"Malia, I won't give you up. I'll get you back, one way or another. You can bet on it." He was angry now, his face flushed, his Adam's apple more prominent than ever.

Malia slid out of her seat, ran out of the bakery, crossed the street, and darted into Misaki's. She disappeared into the back of the store behind a 'no admittance' sign. Asking to use the phone, she quickly dialed the number, her heart pounding.

"George, hello. This is Malia. Can you help me with a little problem? I'd appreciate it if you would meet me in Kalae at the house where we can talk in private."

"Sure, Malia, your wish is my command. How about four in the afternoon?" said the voice one the other end of the line. "I'll be off duty by then."

"Wonderful, Mike should be home shortly after that. You're always invited for pupus. Don't think Jeannie would like it if I kept you past dinnertime."

Laden down with more than a few bags of groceries, Malia struggled to keep them balanced. A few steps from reaching her car door, she accidently bumped into a pedestrian.

"Here, let me help you. You have an armload."

"Thanks so much, I'd like to put them all in my trunk."

"No sooner said than done. I'm Paul Kanga. We met at your show, but you were so busy I doubt if you would remember. It was fabulous by the way."

"Why, thank you. You're new here, aren't you?"

"Well, in a way I am, but not really. I was stationed in Molokai during the war. Stationed out at the airport in the barracks there. Went to the Med in '46. Now I'm back here as the minister of the Good News Church."

"My goodness. Well, you already know my name is Malia Palani. My husband, Mike, is the school superintendent, and our son Mike is a school principal. His brother, Kimo, is a doctor on the island, and Leilani, our youngest, is an artist. My son Mike's home is across the highway from your church."

"Yes, I know. George Kapule came to see me. I heard about two youngsters finding a body at the pier. I guess it was your grandchildren who discovered it. Grisly finding for two youngsters."

"It was terrible, wasn't it? Do you know if they identified it yet?"

"Not that I've heard. Mrs. Palani, what happened to all the two-story buildings? Didn't there used to be a hotel, and even a place to gamble?"

"Yes, you're right, but when the war ended, they tore down all the brothels—that meant the second stories of the buildings. They were about ready to fall down anyway." Malia laughed. "I hope you enjoy your church calling here. Molokai is my home. I love living here, although it wasn't much fun during the war."

"Please call me Paul."

"And as you know, I'm Malia."

"War isn't fun, and I can imagine what it must have been like for all of you who are native to the island. Maybe one day we can sit and talk about it. You saw it from such a different perspective. How old were you then? Seventeen?"

"I was. Twenty-six years ago." She smiled again. "I'm sorry but I have to get my groceries home."

"Nice to see you again," said Paul.

Malia opened her car door, sat in the front seat, slammed the door shut, turned on the motor, put the car in reverse, looked behind her, and moved out of her parking place into non-existent traffic.

Calmed down from her encounter with Joe, the

chance meeting of someone who had been stationed on Molokai during the war brought back a wealth of memories from 1942, when she made her quilt of tears.

Once baby Kimo arrived, Malia spent hours taking care of him, and playing with him. There was a torrential rainstorm, fifty-two inches. *I remember that.* But the war made many other changes, too. Yuki Tanaka, her best friend, was taken off the island along with her family and most other Japanese that lived on Molokai. Yuki had been born on the island.

I wonder what ever happened to her? The military deported all the Japanese. Only one or two of them were given permission to remain, and they had to wear identifying armbands, and adhere to strict military laws.

All the farm workers...different camps for each ethnicity...Hawaiians, Filipinos, the Chinese, Korean and Samoan...working all together in the fields during the day... each group camped separate and apart...none of them friendly during the evenings. Papa told me that.

Everywhere we looked...uniforms...soldiers...sailors. Papa told me more than 3000 military lived here including a brigadier general. I remember Mama and Papa wouldn't even let me go to the grocery store unaccompanied.

Memories seemed to well up inside of Malia, as she continued to think about the war. *All canned food we ate came from Maui...cash...the only thing we could use. No credit at all. Staples were scarce...how hard it was for Papa to find feed for the chicken and cows. Pineapple and eggplant in abundance because they couldn't be shipped. Mama had to buy some before she could purchase anything else. It became a store rule.* Malia laughed out loud.

I'm surprised I still like pineapple after all we had to

eat. Those Filipinos were really clever. The Navy wouldn't allow any fishing offshore...somehow, they managed to have fish to eat. We only had beef. I guess we were lucky to have that. Lord, in '43 the military took over large pieces of ranch and government lands for troop training...five military targets established, if I remember right.

Malia's thoughts remained in wartime memories until she parked the car in her driveway.

Chapter Seven

George Kapule arrived at the Palani home a little after four. Mike was already home, and he greeted him.

"Aloha, George, and welcome."

"Mahalo, Mike," George said as the two shook hands.

Malia brought out a pitcher of iced tea and glasses along with some tempting pupus for them all to enjoy. Once they were all seated in the lanai, George turned to Malia.

"You just didn't invite me over to be sociable. How can I help you?"

"George, you know Joe Obregon is back on the island. I agreed to have a cup of coffee with him, and then he told me he wanted me back. When I said I wasn't interested in any kind of relationship with him, he became angry. I'm scared he's going to do something foolish. His actions frightened me. I'm afraid he might do something violent, either to me, or maybe even to Mike."

"Did he say anything in particular to you?"

"He grabbed my arm and told me he'd get me back one way or another. I had to run out of the bakery and into Misaki's back room to escape him."

"Darling, I didn't realize you had seen him," said Mike.

"I hadn't until this afternoon, but I felt George should know what Joe did. He really frightened me."

Mike walked over to Malia, put his arm around her, and gave her a reassuring hug. "Darling, I'm so sorry. I haven't seen him either except at a distance. I figured he would have nothing to do with the Palanis period."

"I'm glad you brought me into the loop, Malia. For sure I'll keep a closer watch on him," said George.

A few weeks later, George made a return visit to the Palani home.

"Mike, it seems the minister of the Good News Church knows Joe from the Navy. When I first met him, he didn't tell me he knew Obregon even though I mentioned his name. But the town seems to be buzzing with the fact that Joe has been seen in his church, and the minister has been seen on his boat, fishing with him. Joe is also sober, and no one has seen him in any of the bars. Paul Kanga must have some kind of hold on him. They've been as thick as thieves."

"George, I met Paul by accident the same day I had the encounter with Joe. I literally bumped into him and almost dropped all my groceries. He carried them to my car and put them inside for me," said Malia.

"Maybe I should make another trip out to his church and ask if he can shed any light on the subject. It seems mighty strange he didn't tell me he knew Joe."

"Pastor Kanga, Paul, do you have time to talk with me? "

"Of course. George, would you join me in a cup of bad coffee while we talk?"

"Never turn that down. Thanks. It's about Joe Obregon."

"I think I may have misled you inadvertently. You asked me about a Joe Obregon. I literally hadn't thought about or heard that name in twenty years. Yes, I did know a Joe Obregon. We were on the same ship in the Mediterranean. But I hadn't seen him in years. While at the barbershop a few days before I met you, I casually asked the barber if he knew a Joe Obregon who had been in the Navy. Then I was told about him, and I might be able to find him on his boat. Since I knew no one here, I thought maybe he might be the same one, fiery temper, always in trouble. I got out of the Navy in '47, and went to a Bible college in the Midwest. I never expected being a pastor would be my life's calling. But maybe it's like father like son. I've been a pastor for coming up on ten years now. When I saw Joe, I thought maybe I could turn his life around."

The two men sat drinking coffee, and then George dropped the tiny bombshell.

"I guess I should tell you he has been harassing Malia, and she's scared to death he's going to do something violent and stupid. Do you think you might be able to help counteract that?"

"With the Lord's help, lots of prayer, and keeping him away from the booze."

George laughed. "I haven't seen him sober since the day he arrived back on the island."

"Trust me, he is sober now. He told me he wanted to turn his life around. I hope I can believe him. He's been coming to my church even though he's Catholic." Paul wore the mantle of a minister in his actions and deeds. He knew he had become a different man.

"You're a good guy, Paul, and I appreciate the candor."

When George left, Paul sat down again in his chair and put his head in his hands. *I don't know what is going on in my life, but I'm going to help George all I can. I really like being a minister even though I've spent a good part of my life on the dark side. I know I'm changing. I hope God can forgive me for all the sins I've committed.*

Then the new Paul Kanga did something he had never done before: he got down on his knees and prayed.

Chapter Eight

A few weeks passed after the quilting show. The new pastor was settling in. Paul discovered he really enjoyed being a minister and thus began a concerted personal campaign to be as helpful and community involved as possible. One afternoon while sitting in on a Church Women's meeting, Pastor Paul approached the ladies present.

"I heard some very good singing voices in church last Sunday."

The women blushed with appreciation. Paul noticed he was being eyed up and down by one of the ladies. *I'll have to watch that. I don't want any entanglements with the ladies of the congregation.*

The next Sunday, Paul and the congregation were treated to some special music. Once the choir was singing on a regular basis, he asked his congregation for guitar and/or ukulele players. Soon there was music on Sundays. Music rang from the rafters of the church, and the congregation began to increase in size.

Pastor Paul was delighted to discover the man who delivered mail to his church also delivered to Kaulaupapa, the leper colony. He made plans to accompany him on his mule ride at the next scheduled mail delivery. Paul had never seen a leper colony before and was anxious to also meet the priest who lived there. He saw the priest as a godly man who spent his life ministering to the sick and the dying. *Where does he get his strength and energy? Not many men would sacrifice their health and life. I need to talk with him. God has blessed him with a great deal of grace as well as fortitude.*

After his first venture down the mountain with the mule, Paul began making regular visits to talk with the priest, learning from the wisdom he imparted. Paul watched as the priest cared for the lepers and their families. He saw the results of the priest's ministrations and wanted to enhance his own congregation. *Maybe not as dramatic as the priest, but I can help in many ways. I know I can provide blessings and care of a different kind since I've been part of the 'real' world.*

As the months passed, word began to spread about the pastor of the Good News Church. Then Paul's first opportunity to help came about in an unusual way. One Saturday morning, Mike Palani walked across the highway to the front door of the church.

"Pastor, we've never met even though I live across the highway. I'm also principal of the high school."

"Please come in," said Paul holding the door open with his shoulder. He shook hands with his visitor. "I'm Pastor Paul Kanga."

"Mikala, Mike Palani the younger." He sat

down in the chair Paul pointed out to him. "I've seen how good you are with people. I'll get right to the point, Pastor Paul. I wondered if you might be interested in doing some coaching one afternoon a week for one of my boy's teams? I'm in desperate need of a coach for the baseball team. The last pastor who served this church helped until he moved somewhere in the Midwest. I thought maybe you could carry on the tradition."

"I haven't played baseball in years," Paul responded. "Don't know how good I would be. But it sounds like it might be fun to meet some of the younger population on the island. Might keep me in better shape. All this Spam and eggs I've been eating since arriving on the island." He touched his stomach, which had grown from the time he set foot on Molokai. He laughed, and Mike joined in.

"I know how busy pastors can be, Paul, but would three to five on Thursday afternoons fit into your schedule?"

"That's probably the best time you could pick. Choir practice is at seven that night. It would give me an hour to get a bite down. Do I just show up at the school? Do you want me to announce it at my church service I'll be coaching baseball on Thursday afternoons?" Paul was bursting with questions.

"No, not yet. Come to my office at the school, and I'll give you a tour of the facilities. On the day you begin coaching, I'll personally accompany you down to the baseball field."

"Do I need some kind of uniform?"

"We won't worry about that yet. When can you meet me at the office?"

"Would ten Monday morning be too soon?"

"Absolutely not. And my wife Grace will kill me if I come home and haven't asked you to have supper with us tonight." Mike smiled at Paul. "I caught some beautiful Akuli this morning. It will be three adults and our two boys. We do have a vegetable garden so you will get salad. In any case, it will be a simple meal."

"I like those best," Paul said. "I'm not good for anything in the food preparation department except buying groceries to eat at the market. Let me bring ice cream. I know the boys will like that."

"We'll see you around five then."

"I hate to be an eat and run kind of guest but I have a big day on Sunday and will still have to check over my sermon, so I can't stay long."

"No problem, we're just happy to have you as our guest."

"Then I'll be there with my chow bag in place," Paul said laughing as he let Mike out the door.

Maybe Joe will see what I'm doing, and it might mellow him out. I can only pray for that.

On a sunny afternoon with the trade winds blowing on his back, Paul walked along a stretch of beach meditating on all that had been happening to him. He looked up when he heard a cry for help. A young boy was caught in a rip tide. Paul wasted no time in removing his shoes and running into the water. The strong tide was whipping and changing directions. Paul managed to grab the youngster's arm, and he struggled to bring the two of them to shore. Once in calm water, he threw his arms around the boy and walked to the warm sand where he set him down and sat beside him.

"How come you're swimming alone?"

"My friends didn't want to come."

"Don't you know how dangerous Papohaku Beach is? You shouldn't be out here alone. I'm glad I happened to be in the vicinity."

"I'm glad, too," said the boy. He breathed heavily.

"Where do you live? I'll take you home."

"Maunaloa. Please don't tell my mom what happened."

"Son, I can't do that. She'll be grateful to know you're alive and safe."

After taking the tired young man back to his home, Paul drove in his wet clothes back to the rectory. *Sure doesn't matter with this heap on the floor. If nothing hurt it before, a little water won't spoil it any further. I have this strange feeling inside my skin, like I'm a kameleona. Each day, the dark parts of the lizard changes to a light color as if my thoughts are no longer dark, but full of hope and light. I never thought I would enjoy being a minister, but I do. How long can it last before the authorities catch up with me?*

Chapter Nine

Life on Molokai returned to its normal quiet pace. Malia's encounter with Joe appeared to be a one and only occurrence. People couldn't believe their own eyes when they saw Joe with his truck, selling fish in the afternoons on Ala Malama. He was sober and smiling and clean shaven. His hair was also well-groomed. Not the Joe Obregon they had seen a few months before, someone who couldn't stay out of bars, couldn't stay clean, drunk on hard liquor, and passed out on the deck of Joe's Folly, not to wake up for several hours. He had been no one's favorite.

Paul began to wonder if this was any of his doing. He was happy to see Joe in this new state. He even went fishing with Joe several times and came home with enough fish to feed his congregation. Paul knew he felt comfortable in his new preacher skin, and did whatever he could to enhance it. He made visits to the home-bound of his congregation, he started a Bible class. He welcomed congregants to his office, his coffee pot always ready for use. He enjoyed counseling the young people.

George returned several times for coffee at the rectory. He liked the minister and enjoyed his company. One morning as they were having a friendly conversation, George casually asked, "Paul, who else was on the plane when you arrived at the airport?"

"One other passenger, another man, George, and not talkative."

George nodded, and thoughts whirred around. "I know you didn't see the body, but do you think you might be able to describe the man."

Paul sat back on his chair for the moment. "Let's see. About my size and height." He laughed. "Well, I think I've put on a few pounds since I arrived. All the Spam and eggs and rice. I don't think he was Hawaiian, but he had Asian blood. I don't look Hawaiian, but my Dad's last name was Hawaiian. My mother was black Irish. Dark. Think a lot of my coloring came from her. I often thought she might have been a gypsy."

"Well, your lineage isn't important. I'm trying to find the identity of our John Doe. Someone must be missing him."

"Yes, I would suppose so. I wish I could help you more, George."

"It's the daily life of a policeman, pursuing clue after clue. I'm sorry we had to bury the body without identification."

"Sad," Paul agreed.

"The airline manifest lists you, and a man named Jack Metzger."

"At least you have a name now. Was he from

Honolulu? Or was he just changing planes?"

"We know he came from someplace else, but we've run into a dead end."

Paul stood up and went to the sink "I need a drink of water. Could I get a glass for you too?" His heart pounded as he walked towards the kitchen counter.

"Thanks," said George, "but I need to be on my way. Good to talk with you, Paul."

"Same here, George. God be with you," said Paul as he let George out the door.

After George left, Paul walked into his bathroom and splashed his face with water. "Oh, dear God, what will I do next?" He saw his troubled face in the mirror.

The phone rang, and Paul walked into his office to answer it.

"Hello. Yes, Mrs. Sakamoto. I'd be happy to officiate at your daughter's wedding. What is the date? March 3. That fits in with my schedule. Would the happy couple like to come and see me to discuss the service? Wonderful, I'll see them tomorrow afternoon around four then." Paul hung up after marking all the information in his calendar.

His phone rang again. This time the party on the other end wanted him to perform a funeral service for their mother. He agreed, the time was set for Saturday morning, and flyers would be put up around town informing the population of one of his congregant's demise. Paul thought it seemed a strange way to inform people, but this was a small island with an infrequent newspaper.

Paul became enmeshed in church life and activities, and he relished it, something he never expected. How long would it last? He knew he had to leave before the law caught up with him. If anyone from the real Paul Kanga's church came to check up on him—"Oh, Lord, please don't let it happen." He said another silent prayer.

Joe showed up about five o'clock the next day, clean and sober. "How about going deer hunting with me tomorrow?"

"Deer hunting? I don't even own a rifle."

"I've got a couple of old ones on the boat. We can get some ammo."

"Don't we need a permit of some kind?"

"My friend owns a lot of acreage. Guess you could call it a ranch, but he doesn't live there. We can even borrow his jeep."

"Sounds great. I could use a change in my diet." Paul laughed.

"I'll pick you up around six a.m."

Joe arrived behind the wheel of an old Army jeep, its camouflage green color dulled by the years of age and relentless sun and salt air. Paul couldn't help but hear him drive up, the noisy motor sputtering and coughing.

"Maybe to thank your friend for the loan of his jeep, we might tear it apart and fix it," said Paul as he climbed into the front seat.

"That's a good thought." Joe backed the vehicle up and turned onto the highway going west towards Maunaloa. As they passed the airport, Joe made a left-hand turn onto a narrow dirt road and drove until he came to a gated fence.

"Open the gate for me, will you, Paul? And then close it when I pull the jeep inside."

Paul did as he was asked and then climbed back into the jeep. "Oh, look, there's a deer across the field right now."

"Just a baby," said Joe. "I want one of those multi-pronged bucks." He whispered to Paul. "We can leave the jeep here. Don't slam the door. It might scare any deer around."

Paul enjoyed the cool of the morning as they found a good place covered with scrub brush, sedge and the kiave trees on which the deer ate the leaves. They waited hunkered down, hidden by brush. It was almost sundown when a huge six-prong buck walked twenty feet in front of them. The men took careful aim, and Joe had his prize.

"This big guy's got to weigh at least two fifty," said Paul.

"We need to let it hang at the butchers for a week before we can prepare it."

A week later, Joe and Paul began their skinning job on the large Formica table in the rectory kitchen.

"I can show you how to cure the skin if you'd like it for a rug or to hang on the wall."

Paul's face took on a strange look. He put his knife down.

"What's wrong, pastor? Didn't you plan using that knife on the man whose identity you stole? Getting cold feet?" asked Joe.

"No, I didn't, and I'm okay," said Paul. "I'm not comfortable planning a murder, any murder. My conscience already feels guilty. I don't feel like Jack anymore, just Pastor Paul Kanga of the Good News Church."

"Don't forget, buddy, whatever you call yourself, if we get caught, you'll be as guilty as I am."

"I wish I could forget." Paul mumbled to himself. Wanting to change the subject, he looked over at Joe.

Joe sensed his discomfort, but didn't want Jack to forget he knew about the real Paul Kanga, and that George was not going to let up in his search to learn the identity of the body found in the Grove. Thinking about his plan to make Mike Palani disappear, he had another idea. "Hey, do you think your church might like a venison barbecue?"

"What a colossal idea. We can print some flyers and put them up. I know all the ladies would love to bring their favorite dishes. Can we do this on the church lawn, or do you think we should go to a park where there are tables and seats?" Paul was pleased with the idea, and hoped Joe might be changing his mean streak. He liked the Palanis, and continued to think of ways to talk Joe out of his plans.

"Jack, I'd like to invite Mike Palani as a peace offering. I'm going to go over to his office and ask him."

"Please Joe, don't call me Jack again. I'm Paul Kanga, minister, and I'm happy staying that way." Going back to Joe's comment, Paul looked at him. "Do you think that's wise?"

"I don't know, but I would like to begin putting him off guard." Joe saw the troubled look on his friend's face. "Don't forget why I got you here in the first place."

That afternoon, Joe in his new cleaned up appearance went to Mike's office. "I'd like to see Mr. Palani, please."

The office secretary knew it was Joe, so instead of using the phone to tell him Joe wanted to see him, she went to his office. "You shouldn't see him, Mike, not after all the trouble he's caused your family," she whispered softly.

"It's all right. Send him in." Mike stayed behind his desk when Joe entered.

"Hello, Mike. Before you say anything, I'd like to apologize. And that's why I'm here. Pastor Paul and I went hunting and bagged a huge buck. We are having a venison feast for his church after services on Sunday. I wanted to invite you and Malia to show you I have no hard feelings."

Mike just stared at the man across from him for several seconds before he spoke. His body had an uncomfortable visceral reaction, but he maintained a calm façade. "Joe, your gesture and apology are accepted, but no, Malia and I won't be at the church feast."

The conversation between the two men was very stilted. Finally, Joe said, "let me at least bring you a couple of pieces of venison. It makes great hamburgers."

"That's kind of you." Mike wasn't at all certain as to what to make of Joe's gesture.

"I'll bring it to your house."

"No, I don't think so, Joe. Bring it to my office. I'm here till about four every afternoon, Monday through Friday."

"If that's what you want." Joe managed to keep his tone civil. He smiled at Mike.

The conversation was interrupted by a young man stepping into Mike's office. "Hi, Dad. Thought you might like to go kayaking with me, tomorrow about nine?" Young Mike then noticed Joe in the office. "Oh, sorry Dad, didn't know you had someone here."

"It's okay, Mike. He and I have finished our business." The father did not introduce Joe or tell his son who he was. He figured Mike might already knew Joe was his birth father.

"I'll bring the venison by tomorrow. It was truly good to see you again." Joe hoped he sounded humble. He wasn't about to screw up his great plan.

True to his word, Joe brought the venison the next day. Mike was in a conference, so Joe left it with his secretary. When he left Mike's office, he felt so parched, he wanted to go have a beer in the bar. But he knew he couldn't if he wanted all his plans to go right. He hopped into his truck, and decided to drive out to the east end of the island. He hadn't been there in years. The road was still as bad as ever. The truck bounced and shimmied, but Joe made it beyond the bridge. He parked the truck along the road on a sandy siding, and slid out of the driver's seat.

It seems so peaceful now. I can remember when all I could see were concrete bunkers and soldiers. Geez, the last time I was here was with Mike and Kimo Pascua when we decided we'd canoe to Honolulu. That water looks so inviting.

Seeing he was hidden from the road where he stood on the sand, Joe stripped, set his clothes down on a large boulder and dived into a deep pocket. *God, I'd love to have a place on this part of the island.* He stretched his arms up to the sky. He walked back towards the shore as waves curled over the rocks, the white foam pluming upwards, crashing back again. Joe emerged from the water, shook himself dry, put his jeans and shirt back on, and sat down on the boulder. He pulled out a cigarette from his shirt pocket, lit it, and took a deep, satisfying drag. The ocean had a mesmerizing effect on him, and he let his mind wander. *"Maybe I could get Mike to go hiking with me. In these hills at the top, it's not safe. Maybe he could lose his footing. Maybe I could try to save him and couldn't. Lots of maybes. I'll have to think about that.*

The tide was coming in, and Joe, not wanting to get caught sitting in the water, stood up, took one last look at the scene in front of him, then returned to his truck. On the way back, he stopped at a little roadside stand for a cold drink. He was paying for his soda, when he and the clerk kept looking at each other.

"I think I know you," said the clerk. "We competed in the Makahiki games. It must have been years ago."

"If we did, it was a lot of years ago. Nice to see you," Joe mumbled without introducing himself, and left.

The ride back to town was uneventful, but to Joe it was reliving history. When he finally parked his car on the dock near his boat, his mood was melancholy. He wanted company. He climbed back into his truck and drove to the Church of Good News. The dilapidated car was in the driveway.

"Paul," he called. "Come have a hamburger with me. My treat."

Paul was sitting at his desk, busy writing, and checking text from what Joe thought was a Bible. "I have to finish my sermon for Sunday, Joe. What time is it?"

"After six. How much more do you have to do?" His tough demeanor seemed to be disappearing as his body fidgeted while he stood talking to Paul.

Sensing Joe's agitation, Paul said, "Can you give me about ten minutes more? There's a new Life magazine you can look at in the meantime."

"Yeh, I can do that." Joe sat down in the old

leather chair opposite Paul's desk with the magazine in hand.

Later, as they sat enjoying their burgers and fries, Joe looked at Paul. "I know how to make that certain person disappear."

Paul looked at Joe, started to ask a question, then thought better of it.

"Do you know the east end of the island?" Joe continued.

Paul nodded.

"Well, it's a great place to hike, lots of trails, waterfalls, and high drop off points on the cliffs if you get my meaning."

"Joe, I don't want to talk about any of this in a public place. Let's go for a drive, or you can come back to the rectory, or we can go sit on your boat."

Paul's stomach felt queasy as he thought about Joe's idea. *How can I stop it? If I go to George Kapule, will Joe tell him my real identity? It will take Joe time to get Mike to even trust him to go hiking. I hope it will give me a little time to figure things out.*

Chapter Ten

Life continued at its leisurely pace on Molokai. Children were born. Old people died. Over three years had passed since Paul and Joe had their dinner conversation. Mike, Paul, Joe, and George were now kayaking together each weekend, and the tension between Mike and Joe seemed to be lessening. Mike and Joe never discussed Malia, or anything relating to the Palani family. Paul prayed and hoped Joe's plans were also far and away from his mind and dissipating as time wore on.

The death of the real Paul Kanga lay heavy on his heart. *I know I'll have to atone for it. It's inevitable George will find out. I don't know what the penalty is for assuming another's identity. The fact that I tried to dispose of the body instead of reporting it, I probably made a heap of trouble for myself. Should I confess to him?* Jack Metzger's secret burned a hole in his gut.

Paul had fit into the community of Kaunakakai. He was loved by his church congregation, and membership had been growing. He knew he had turned his life around. He thought about Joe. Was it all an act? Paul was afraid he knew the answer. Joe's outward actions belied his innermost thoughts. No one could say Joe was the same person he was three years ago. Only Paul knew his hidden agenda, and that gave him great concern. Joe had even put in an appearance at St. Sophia in the last year. Since everyone seemed welcoming, he continued to attend mass there, even though he and Paul remained good friends.

Joe's income from the fish he caught began to give him a small nest egg. One afternoon, a man who chartered his boat for a day of fishing told him he had a small piece of property on the east end he wanted to sell.

"It was my Dad's land. But he's been dead since before the war, and Mom has no desire to live on it."

Joe grinned from ear to ear as he listened to the man who had chartered his boat. "Do you mean you really want to sell it?" Joe's smile grew wider and wider.

"I'd like to."

"Could we take a ride out to see it after we get back to the dock? We can use my truck if you don't mind the fish smell," Joe said as he laughed.

"Sure. Riding in a fish truck will be a new experience for me."

"Have you seen the property before?" Joe asked.

"Yes, but I was a lot younger. I do remember there's a little road on the south side of the main road just past a little food store. Maybe the store isn't there anymore."

"Oh, it's there all right. It's been there since the

stone age I think." Joe laughed. He couldn't believe his good fortune. It was the same area where he took his impromptu swim. The man was willing to sell at a price Joe could afford.

Once all the paperwork was completed and money changed hands, Joe moved in. Void of any furniture, it started to look more like a home when congregation members from Paul's church donated a bed and couch, and someone gave him an old stove.

"I can't even begin to describe the feeling," Joe told Paul when he came to see the new place. "I even have hot and cold running water and an inside shower."

"Right on the water, and so private, I imagine you can skinny dip here all you want."

"That's true, I've already done it. In fact, I did so before I even knew the property was available."

"You're a lucky guy, Joe. Don't blow it now."

Joe's face flared with anger, but he kept quiet and said nothing.

"I'll be leaving now, hope to see you in church on Sunday," said Paul. He made a quick retreat, as he didn't want to be a recipient of Joe's temper.

Over the next few months, Joe continued to fish off the Folly and sell his catch. When he wasn't fishing, he was improving his little cottage by the sea. As time went by, he became handier and handier with building projects. He stood outside his front door one day and looked over all he had accomplished.

I can't believe I've done all this. The only thing my little hale needs now is a new coat of paint on the inside.

When he was in the hardware store purchasing paint, Paul was there on an errand for the church. "Hi Paul, long time no see. I'm getting ready to paint the inside of my house. I could use some help."

Since little communication had gone on between them, Paul was eager to assist his friend. "I can get a couple of the younger guys in my church to come help, too. That is, if you would like it."

"The more the merrier. I'll get finished faster, too."

The outside house colors Joe had chosen were a gray blue for the frame, and bright white for the trim. The front door was painted a dark blue.

"Joe, you've been hiding out on me. This looks like someone came in and helped you." Paul and his buddies couldn't believe the outside looked so good. "Great looking paint job," Paul told him. "You've been working your butt off, man."

"Well, it's the inside that needs the work. And I'm grateful for the help." Joe smiled at the three men. "Of course, you haven't seen the inside yet. No digs please. I'm working on it." He gave a friendly laugh. "I ordered some real furniture from Sears, so I want everything to be painted clean before I pick it up at the dock. Young's is bringing it over from Honolulu on their next run to Molokai. My order filled one half of a container."

"You must have bought out the furniture department," said Paul.

"No, just half of it, some new appliances and some rugs," he joked. "Now let's talk about this paint job. I thought if the walls were painted light sandy beige with white trim, that would be something simple to do, and the color will look like the beach."

"Whatever you say, you're the boss." All the men laughed. "I brought some sandwich fixings to keep us going while we're working."

"Thanks. Just stuff it in the fridge."

It was a successful day for all of them. The inside was completely painted. The men Paul brought got to see Joe in a completely different light. Paul hoped it was a good sign Joe might be softening on his 'get Mike' mission.

Chapter Eleven

Mother and daughter had little time together as Leilani had been on the mainland attending art school in Los Angeles. Malia decided she and Leilani should go to Papohaku Beach, where Leilani could paint, and Malia could lie in the shade and read or swim in the shallow water. A beautiful Tuesday morning, with soft trade winds and blue skies, they were excited about their day trip.

"Mom, you've packed enough food to feed an army. Don't forget we have to carry it down to the sand."

"We could do that, but I thought we should sit in the park nearby, enjoy our lunch and not have to haul it anywhere."

Leilani nodded in agreement. As they were driving on the road towards the beach, the right rear tire on Malia's car blew out. Unable to control the sudden jolt, the car careened into a ditch. Leilani, thrown from the passenger seat, fell to the ground. By the time someone saw the car and its passengers, Malia managed to wrest herself from the car through the window. Someone called an ambulance. Malia rode with Leilani as it sped towards the clinic.

"Mom, I'm so sorry, our special day was ruined."

"I'm just grateful we're both alive. Dad told me the tire was in shreds when he saw it."

"Did Kimo tell you how long I have to be in this cast? I can't take care of my apartment or the cat or anything."

"Those are easy answers, darling, at least the last ones. You will come to stay in our home, in your old room, and you can bring Pookie with you. She's an indoor cat mostly, there'll be no problem."

"But I can't have you waiting on me hand and foot."

"Oh, yes you can. I'll love having you home again. If I need more help I'll ask Grace to pitch in. Your leg is broken in two places. You're lucky there were no more injuries. You could have been killed."

"I know, Mom. I'm grateful to be alive. But when I think about my sister-in-law, she has two active boys to take care of plus Mike. She has her hands full."

"Don't give me those buts, Leilani. We'll just go with the flow."

"Yes, Mother," she said with a sheepish grin.

Pookie made herself happily at home on Leilani's bed, her fluffy orange tail curled up and her head under Leilani's arm. She helped entertain Leilani while her leg healed.

Leilani was ecstatic when she could join her family at dinner and sit at the table, her leg propped up on a stool. She sat sideways, allowing her leg to lie straight.

"I have some interesting news," said Mike, taking a bite of fish. "I've hired a new teacher."

"What will she teach, Dad?"

"The teacher is a he, and he will teach math and phys ed. One thing unusual about him is that he is a wood carver. That's why he came back to Hawaii. He loves the wood here."

"Oh," said Leilani, her interest piqued. "What's his carving like?"

"He is a true artist, Leilani. I saw some of his work when I gave him the offer. I'd like to invite him to dinner."

"When?" asked Malia.

"Tomorrow night, if that's okay with you, honey. Please don't fix anything spectacular, hamburgers would be great."

"Well, I don't want to serve those, but do invite him. What's his name? And tell us about him."

"His name is Keanu Emery. He was born on Oahu, but went off to college in Oregon, and stayed there after he graduated."

"What made him decide to come back?" asked Leilani, her ears perking up at the thought of someone new in Kaunakakai.

"Well, as I said, he loves to carve wood. He told me that although redwood is beautiful, he prefers koa or milo. Can't get those in Oregon."

"How old is he?"

"Am I detecting some interest here, Leilani?" Her father laughed. "He's two years older than you, if that satisfies you. And he is good looking. Full blooded Hawaiian, rugged face, well-built physique, brown skin, black hair. Yes, I think you will like him, my dear."

"Dad, stop teasing me. Just because I haven't met anyone I'd like to marry…" She trailed her sentence off. "Dinner will be interesting." She got up from the table, took her crutches, and slowly maneuvered her body into the living room, where she had a book waiting for her. But Leilani's mind wasn't on any book, no matter how interesting.

The next evening, Leilani sat in the living room waiting for their dinner guest. She had washed her hair, and brushed it till it shone. She put on her prettiest muumuu. It hid her leg cast. In her hair, she attached a yellow hibiscus behind her ear.

"You look beautiful, Leilani," said Malia. *I pray this young man might be someone she will like and maybe grow to love.*

Dinner was a lively affair, with an abundance of Kalbe ribs, rice, and sautéed chard. A non-stop conversation between Keanu and Leilani continued throughout dinner.

"Where did you go to high school? College? Who taught you to carve?" Leilani peppered him with questions.

Malia noticed his good manners, and that he used only a knife and fork to eat the ribs. "Fingers were made before forks, Keanu. Use them, otherwise you'll miss a lot of the good meat on the bones."

"Ribs are my favorite. Can't buy these where I lived before. My parents live in Bend now, and when I went home, Mom always had them for me. Thank you, Mrs. Palani."

"Please, call me Malia."

Chapter Twelve

"Leilani, this is Keanu." Leilani had answered the phone next to where she sat in the living room. A happy smile appeared on her face as she heard a male voice on the phone.

"Hello, Keanu, how are you?" Leilani asked. "How's the teaching treating you?" Keanu had been teaching for about two months.

"To answer you, I'm just fine. I'm enjoying the classes I'm assigned to teach. At least I can say that while it's still new." He laughed. "Leilani, on Sunday afternoon, would you have coffee with me out at the plantation? I can pick you up."

"I'd love to, and if you can drive, I would be grateful. It still is difficult for me to get around. Did you know they have music Sunday afternoons?"

"No, I didn't, but that would make it a lot more fun. I'll pick you up around one, if that's okay. We can have a sandwich, sit, listen to the music and talk."

"I'd like that. See you tomorrow."

"Have you been able to find a place to do your carving?" They sat on the deck of the coffee plantation enjoying their food and listening to the haunting island sounds of a guitar and ukulele.

"As a matter of fact, I heard yesterday about a place for rent close to town. I'm told it has a large enclosed lanai. Sounds like a great place to set up a studio, and have all my carving materials in one place."

"If you want it, you better grab it now. Rentals are really difficult to find, especially close to town."

"It's so close to the school I can ride a bike if I want."

"That will give you some exercise, not that you'll need any more after your PE classes." Leilani wiped the edges of her mouth with a napkin as the sauce from her pork sandwich left a telltale mark around her lips. "Yum, this tastes great. Don't you want a bite?" she asked Keanu.

"I've plenty to eat with this giant hamburger. I'm glad we came. The guy who plays the guitar and that ukulele player are really good."

"Wait till you hear the man that sings. His voice is wonderful." *I'd love to have him sing at my wedding*, she thought.

I really do like Leilani—more than like her. I think I could easily fall in love with her, Keanu thought.

"When your leg is healed, we can start playing some tennis."

"I'd like that, although I'm certain you're going to have to give me some lessons. I haven't played in a long time."

"My pleasure, Leilani."

"Would you like me to go with you to see this place you're thinking of renting?" Leilani said. "We can go after we leave here."

"It's on Beach Place."

"I love that street."

Once Keanu signed the rental papers and paid his deposit, he moved his belongings into the main part of the house, and took all his carving materials out to the enclosed lanai. Glad to have Leilani to help him, he checked all the corners and roof to make certain no untoward rain could come through and ruin his work.

"You have a find here, Keanu," she said.

"I know. Maybe I can convince you to come over and paint while I carve."

"That would be fun. You'll have to bring over my easel for me. In this condition, I can't carry anything as bulky as that."

Keanu laughed. "I think you'll have to carry it," he said making a joke. "Would next weekend be too soon?"

The following Saturday, Leilani is sat in Keanu's studio with a large canvas in front of her, her palette in one hand and a brush in the other. However, what engrossed her thoughts more surrounded Keanu busy carving a canoe out of Koa wood. Although no verbal communication passed between them, a frisson of happiness surrounded the two of them.

Keanu stopped carving, put his knife down, and stood, stretching his arms up and sideways rolling his shoulders. He looked at Leilani, and made a contented sound. "Lani, I need a break. Want to take a short walk downtown with me?"

"Sounds good. Let me finish the shading on these leaves, I just got the mixture to the colors I want. Then I can stick my brushes into water before they stiffen."

As they walked up Mohala Street to cross the highway, Keanu commented on all the chickens in the bushes.

"They're here all the time," said Leilani. "Get used to the clucking." She laughed.

"No problem, Lani. By the way, I've been asked by the kids to chaperone the dance next Saturday night. Would you like to come with me?"

"That would be fun. You must be a very popular teacher, Mr. Emery."

"I'm not so certain about that. But I am one of the youngest. And I think your Dad trusts me to be a diligent chaperone."

"I know he does."

As Keanu danced the Twist and the Watusi with Leilani, she couldn't believe what great rhythm he had. Leilani much preferred the slow dances. *I love it when Keanu holds me close.* The dance floor jumped to the sound of Chubby Checker. "I can't twist another minute; can we please sit down? You're so much a better dancer than I am."

"But, honey, I couldn't ask for a better partner." Keanu excused himself, leaving Leilani alone for a few minutes. When he returned, he sat down next to Leilani and whispered in her ear. "Some of the kids might not like this teacher after tonight. I found their stash of beer."

"Oh, Lord, what kids won't try to get away with. What did you do with the beer?"

"It's all locked up in Mike's office." Keanu tried to keep a straight face as he told Leilani.

"He'll get a big surprise when he walks in on Monday morning." Leilani couldn't help but laugh at the picture she conjured up in her head, her brother walking into his office, a room full of beer bottles.

After the dance, Keanu and Leilani stopped on the way back to Keanu's they stopped at the ice cream store for a big cone. "Sorry your car is at my place, otherwise I would drive you home."

"It's okay, Keanu. It's not far."

Keanu put his arms around her, and gave her a large kiss, and several smaller kisses showering her face. Leilani eagerly returned his affection. She felt they both wanted more, but she didn't want to be the aggressor.

As Leilani drove home, she thought about the time she spent with Keanu. Leilani knew she was falling in love with him and hoped he felt the same way. When she climbed into bed that night, she sighed, and Pookie made herself comfortable in the crook of her arm. *Wish you were Keanu.* She drifted off to sleep.

Over the next few months, no one saw Joe Obregon drunk or with a drink in his hand. Paul thought maybe he had given up his idea to get Mike Palani. But the next time he saw Joe, he reiterated his plan again.

"Did you ever have a chance to hike on the east side of the island?" Joe asked Paul.

"No, the only thing I did was patrol the roads, and check the bunkers."

"Next week, come on a hike with me, in the afternoon would be good. We can hike, take a swim, and I will barbecue something for dinner."

"Sounds like a plan," Paul said. "Thursday would be good for me."

Joe and Paul were caravanning down the highway. Joe had his catch of fish in the ice chests in the bed of his truck, and Paul chugged along in the old Packard.

"We'll take the jeep," Joe said as he walked over to Paul, "I want to show you some really beautiful property."

The 'so called' bridge over the inlet water was rickety at best. The road wasn't much better. But the scenery was magnificent with the big trees and their overlapping limbs, the ocean splashing against the white rocks. Once Joe had driven through the forest thicket, he came to a section of the island where the land was green and fertile, and just waiting to be planted and cultivated.

"What's out here?" asked Paul.

"This is Halawa Valley where an entire community lives without indoor plumbing electricity and without gas or water lines. See that lean-to on the left? That's usually a home for one or two, or even a family."

"With all the modern conveniences available, this area seems pretty old fashioned for when you think about it."

"It's never changed, not even after the war. It's like time stood still. These people like living off the land. Molokai truly has its own counterculture. Whatever you want to call these people, they still hunt the wild boar, fish the water, and grow their veggies. Look at the field over there on our left. Its taro root, sweet potatoes, corn, and maybe some other root vegetables. There's even a small church out here. Food and wildlife are abundant, just for the taking." Joe parked the jeep on a strip of dry land and hopped out.

"C'mon, Paul, I'll take you up to the waterfall."

Joe led with Paul following up the narrow path, through the taro root plantings, and onto a trail with large-leafed plants growing on either side. The trail headed upward. The two of them could hear rushing water.

"I'm astonished. I would never have known a waterfall existed here. I didn't even know there was a waterfall anywhere on the island."

"We'll take the easy trail up to the falls. They are really something to see."

Four hours later, an energized Paul arrived back at the beach house with Joe. Paul noticed how very tired Joe looked even though they wanted to take a swim. They stripped and dived into the blue water.

"That water feels great. I'd love to swim every day."

"You bet. I try to if I'm not too tired." answered Joe. "Would you like a beer?"

"I'd rather have some iced tea if you have it."

"Coming up my friend."

Paul drank more than three glasses of iced tea, before he felt his thirst quenched. Noticing how tired Joe seemed to be, he said, "Joe, that's some pretty good looking akule you caught today. Suppose I get about four of them from the fridge, clean them up, and barbecue them on that new grill of yours."

"I'm beat after that long swim and hike. I'll be glad to have you take over cooking duties. You can find some tomatoes on the counter you can slice. I have bread, and butter in the fridge. Will that fill you up?"

"It sounds like a feast, Joe. I'll have to leave right after we eat, though. I have a busy, busy day tomorrow. I've really enjoyed this though. Thanks."

"I know you saw the hills above the falls. I was thinking we could walk out to the end of the land, and climb up from there. It doesn't look too treacherous. And I think I could manage to lure Mike to the edge."

Paul remained quiet. He wanted to say something, but the words just didn't come. He felt whatever he said to Joe would only exacerbate his feelings, nothing to ameliorate. *I've got to do something. Joe looks very tired. I think something might be wrong with him. I know he's not drinking, and he isn't using drugs.*

A few weeks later, Joe found Paul in his office at the rectory.

"Paul, I really want your help. You're my only friend, and so I need to be able to count on you."

"Joe, is something wrong?" Paul could tell from the look on Joe's face it wasn't any simple request.

"Remember how tired I was after our hike?"

"Yes, but I didn't think too much about it since you'd been out fishing most of the day."

"Physically, I think something is wrong with me. I don't seem to have control over my arms or legs. Some days it's worse than others. I never have enough energy. I can't wait to crawl into bed at night. Sometimes I fall asleep on the couch and never make it to the bedroom. Have you noticed the way I walk?" Without waiting for an answer Joe continued. "My gait has changed, and I walk like a cripple."

"What do you want me to do? Go with you to see Kimo?"

"Hello, no. That's the last thing I want to do.

He may be my kid, but I don't want him for my doctor. I want to go to Honolulu and see a specialist of some kind. Would you go with me?"

"Isn't that a little harsh? He's a fine doctor."

"Yes, I know, but I would like to keep all my doctoring away from any of the Palanis."

"Of course I would go to Honolulu with you, Joe. I just must be back in Kaunakakai on Sunday morning for my sermon. If you give me a few days' notice, I can clear the church calendar."

"We'll take Joe's Folly over after church on Sunday. I'm sure we'll be back no later than Thursday. I spoke with the nurse for the doctor I'm seeing. She says I'll need a series of tests. The boat is too uncomfortable to sleep on, but there's a nice cheap hotel, on the Ala Wai Canal. I'll pay for everything."

The two of them wound up staying until Saturday because of the battery of tests the doctor ordered. Joe and Paul were on their way to get the results from the doctor when Joe thought he saw the Palanis.

"Paul, let's get around the corner quick. The Palanis are walking down the street. I don't want them seeing us. People will start asking questions as to why we're here." Joe was a nervous wreck by the time he and Paul were in the doctor's office.

"I know, Joe, but we are doing nothing wrong. It's okay. We're allowed to be in Honolulu." Paul tried to reassure Joe.

The street they turned on housed Joe's doctor in one of the buildings. Paul knew how anxious Joe was to see him before they left Oahu. Joe's anxiety only grew before he was called in to the doctor's office.

"Can my friend come in with me?"

"That's probably a good idea" The doctor sat back in his chair, and waited for the two men to sit down. "Joe, I'm very glad you came to see me. Truthfully, you should have come sooner."

"How bad is it, Doc?"

"One never likes to be the bearer of bad tidings. I know you're sober now, but you've been killing yourself with all the alcohol, pickling your liver to be exact. Any more drinking binges and you might not wake up."

"I can stop, I think."

"True friends won't let you drink another drop." The doctor looked at Paul.

"I'll see he becomes an avid iced-tea drinker, with or without the passion fruit." Paul spoke somberly.

"Unfortunately, that's not your only problem, Joe. The tests I took seem to indicate you may have an early onset of Parkinson's disease."

"What will happen to me?" Joe blanched. "That's a death sentence kind of disease, isn't it?"

"From my preliminary findings, I'm not saying you do have it. But I want you back here in less than a month so I can retest you."

"Thanks for coming with me again to Honolulu." It had been a little over a month since Joe and Paul made their first visit to the doctor. They were ushered into the doctor's office.

"Hello, Joe, how are you feeling today?"

"I have to say my body feels a little weak, I don't know what's wrong, but I can't make it do what I want it to. It's been harder to fish because the lines feel heavier than usual, and it takes me a long time to lay anchor, or pull it up, or even reel in."

"Joe, I'm saddened to tell you it's not going to get any better. Every indication you have given me says you are experiencing full-blown Parkinson's, and from what you are telling me, it's progressing quickly.",

Paul looked at Joe, and he could see the unhappiness in his face. "Joe, I'll do all I can to help you. Doctor, what is Joe going to need?"

"He's probably going to require the use of a cane soon. Can you help him on his boat?"

"I'm a minister, Doctor. I probably could give him a couple of afternoons or mornings a week, but I have my congregation to think of, too." He turned to Joe. "Joe, would that help you out?"

"I'd be grateful Paul for whatever you can do."

A stunned Joe and a sad Paul left the doctor's office and made their way back to the boat.

In spite of Joe's illness, Paul sent up a silent prayer of thank you because Joe wouldn't be able to carry out his plan.

Chapter Thirteen

Leilani and Keanu were seeing each other on almost a daily basis. And if they weren't together, the phone calls were burning up the lines. Keanu took a long lease on the house with the studio, and he and Leilani went hiking every few weeks to find more wood for carving. On weekends, they played records and danced in the evening. Once in a while they went to the movies in Maunaloa.

Keanu began selling his carvings at the Saturday market. Leilani thought his work was beautiful, and wanted him to take some to Honolulu and show the galleries. "Keanu, that's a magnificent little table you are carving. When you're done, I'd like to put it in my gallery and try to sell it for you," she said. "That is if you would like me to," she added.

"Lani, I would really like that. You know how hard it is teaching, then coaching and finding time to carve, and then trying to sell my work. Marketing is not my field. I think my work is better than anything sold at the Saturday market, if I do say so myself."

Leilani smiled at him. "Yes, I agree." She put her arms around him and gave Keanu a warm hug.

One evening after dinner at Keanu's, Leilani stood at the kitchen sink washing their dinner dishes. Keanu came up behind her and put his arms around her. "You feel so good, Lani." He turned her around, wet hands and all, and began stroking her breasts through the shirt she was wearing. Then Keanu removed her shirt and unclasped her bra. Leilani's body just seemed waiting for his touch. His mouth softly grasped one of her nipples. The noises coming from Leilani's mouth told him she wanted more than the kisses they were exchanging. First, he tongued one nipple, then the other. Leilani's body quivered. Keanu removed his shirt, picked up Leilani, cradled her in his arms, and carried her to his bedroom after first locking the front door. Both of them were ravenous for each other. The two of them lay locked together on the bed. Keanu put his arms around her, moving her long hair to the back of her head. He took his tongue and began exploring Leilani's body, licking her tawny skin up one side and down the other. He could feel the wet between her thighs, and took his finger to explore her most inner parts after caressing her neck and bare shoulders. He slipped off her underpants. Leilani unbuttoned Keanu's Levis with his help. Their kisses were passionate and nonstop. He buried his face in her breasts.

"Oh, Lani, you are so beautiful."

Leilani's response was to put her hand in his groin. Keanu slid his tongue down her body until he found and explored between her thighs again. He couldn't get enough of her as he tasted her very essence. Leilani felt like she was on fire, her cries of delight brought her body to a fever pitch. Her body writhed as she clutched Keanu's back with her hands. Keanu's body responded to her sounds, and he grabbed her butt cheeks and with full force entered her. "I'm far too gone to hold out any longer."

"Oh, my God, oh, my God, you feel so good, Keanu."

As their bodies melded into each other, Leilani moaned in delight. Rocking together, the climax came quickly for the two of them.

"I don't want to stop, Lani, but we'll never get any work done if we keep this up." Keanu laughed and hugged her.

The two young lovers lay spent on the bed. "Next time, I'll manage more foreplay. I wanted you so bad, I couldn't wait any longer."

Leilani laughed. "I guess the feeling was mutual."

"Lani, we've been dating for about a year. I don't want anyone but me to be with you. I want you for my wife." He kissed her again. "How do you think your parents would feel about a wedding? I'm not letting you get away from me, girl."

"I think everyone would be very happy." With Leilani's response they embraced each other again and began exploring each other's bodies with as much fervor as the first time.

"Lani, I can't get enough of you. Next weekend, we'll go to Honolulu and find you a ring," said Keanu. "When would you like to get married?"

"When you have a vacation from teaching.

Then we can go on a nice honeymoon."

"Perfect. Christmas is the next one. I'll have two weeks as you know. Where would you like to go?"

"Somewhere on the mainland, I think. I know it will be cold, but have you ever been to Carmel? That's in California. We could fly to San Francisco, spend a few days there, rent a car, and drive down the coast to Carmel. It's an artist's paradise, and I think you would love it."

"That's what we will do then."

"Christmas is only a few months away. I will have a lot to do. When we go to Honolulu, I think I'd better look for a wedding dress, or some fabric to have one made."

"Let's go see your mom and dad, and tell them the news. Knowing your mom, she'll want to do a lot for the wedding, too."

Chapter Fourteen

Leilani and Keanu sat holding hands in the Palani living room.

"I'm so thrilled and excited for the two of you. I know you just got engaged, but have you made any plans at all?" asked Malia.

"The first thing we are going to do is head for Honolulu to buy Leilani a ring. Lani also wants to look at wedding dresses."

"Mom, Keanu and I would love to have you and Dad come along."

Mike had been sitting quietly, taking all the conversation in when he stood up.

"All right, you two, Mom and I would love to fly over to Oahu with you on one condition."

"What's that sir?" inquired Keanu.

"That the two of you let us buy you a good dinner before we return home."

"You're on, Mike. Thank you."

"We'll all have such a good time. Thanks, Mom. Thanks, Dad." Leilani leaned over and kissed Keanu. "Don't you agree, honey?"

"Have you thought about where and when you'd like to get married?" Malia was afraid Leilani would want to be married in the Grove, and all she could think of were sad memories. She breathed a sigh of relief when she heard her daughter's answer.

"I haven't talked it over with Keanu, but would you let us be married here in the garden? It's always so beautiful, and if the ceremony happened at sunset, I couldn't imagine anything more perfect."

"Done, done, and done," exclaimed Malia with delight.

"Have you thought about a wedding date?" asked Mike.

"Well, we thought the day Christmas vacation starts. It won't interfere with Keanu's schedule at school. Then the next day we wanted to fly to San Francisco for our honeymoon, drive down the coast to Carmel. Keanu has never been there, and it is so filled with art and artists, I thought he and I would really love it."

"As long as you are by my side, I can think of nothing more wonderful," Keanu said, squeezing her hand he had been holding. "When can we go shopping? Malia? Mike? Would you be able to get away this weekend?"

"I think we could manage that," said Mike, grinning from ear to ear. "We have to do whatever we can to move this wedding along. There's an eight o'clock plane on Saturday morning."

"Keanu and I can drive to the airport now, and see if we can get tickets. We'll be back in an hour. I'll get the latest return flight that I can."

"Come back here, then I'll have dinner waiting," said Malia.

Saturday morning found the four of them in downtown Honolulu.

"Leilani, I think the best place to look for a dress or fabric would be at Liberty House," said Malia.

"Then that's where we will go. Must be a jewelry store around there where Keanu and Dad can look for a ring for me."

"Good idea, honey. Then we can meet for late lunch, or early dinner at the Royal Hawaiian. Malia, suppose Keanu and I meet the two of you at three. That will give us a few hours before we need to get to the airport," said Mike.

They were leisurely walking down Kalakaua Avenue when Malia nudged Mike.

"Mike," she whispered, "is that Joe with Paul Kanga?"

"You're right, ipo, but I don't have any wish to talk with them. They're going down that side street now. Good. We can avoid any confrontation."

Malia was glad to see them walking away.

Chapter Fifteen

Wedding plans were now in full swing. Leilani was enjoying all the attention and was pleased with the dress she chose a few months before. She had been off island so much the past few years, she only asked one person, a young woman who attended art school with her, to be her honor attendant. Leilani's dress was white organza with white organza flowers dappling the skirt and short train. Leilani desired a crown of stephanotis for her headpiece. She did not want a veil. Because it was the Christmas season, she would carry white peonies with red roses dotted with ferns. Darlene, her maid of honor, would be wearing white organza with a red sash and carrying a bouquet of red roses, with soft white flowers accenting the roses.

"After all, Mom, it is Christmas." The two of them had a good laugh.

Her brothers would be Keanu's best man and usher. They were also responsible for the luau after the ceremony.

Malia hired a crew of women to help her make all the salads and poke. The bakery made a huge wedding cake, since the entire town of Kaunakakai received an invitation to share in the festivities. Long tables would be covered with tapa cloth and decorated with ti leaves. Light from white and red candles would cast a glow everywhere.

When Leilani awoke on her wedding day, it was sprinkling. *It can't rain for my wedding. Everything will be ruined.* About 3:30 in the afternoon, Leilani walked outside and saw the rain had stopped. The sun was shining and, within the next hour, it was dry. She breathed a sigh of relief.

As the sun sank into the blue Pacific, Leilani and Keanu were pronounced husband and wife. Keanu kissed her and didn't want to let go. Leilani's favorite island singer was singing Ke Kali Nei Au, the Hawaiian wedding song, accompanied by his own ukulele music. His voice carried out over the Palani garden.

> *This is the moment*
> *I've waited for.*
> *I can hear my heart singing.*
> *Soon bells will be ringing.*
> *This is the moment*
> *Of sweet Aloha.*
> *I will love you longer than forever.*
> *Promise me that you will leave me never.*
> *I will love you longer than forever.*
>
> *Now that we are one,*
> *Clouds won't hide the sun.*
> *Blue skies of Hawaii smile*

On this our wedding day.
I do love you
With all my heart.

Leilani was beaming. The music was beautiful, and just for her.

"I'm so happy, Lani," Keanu said. "I know we'll have a wonderful life together. I think your mom is looking for you. See her waving at you. I'm going over and visit a bit with my mom and dad. Come and join us as soon as you can."

"Keanu, Leilani is beautiful. I hope you will be bringing her to Bend, so we can have a party for you there," his mother said.

"Not this year, Mom, maybe next summer when I'm not teaching."

"Son." His father's voice had an ominous sound. "Your mom and I have heard rumors around Bend we're not happy about. It seems some woman named Charlene is spreading stories about you and her. She's told everyone she comes in contact with she heard you were on Molokai. She's saying she's moving to Molokai and won't leave until you return to Bend with her. She said you told her you loved her, and wanted to marry her."

"Good lord, Dad. I knew someone in college named Charlene Harper. I dated her twice, found her one of the most obnoxious women on the campus. She actually proposed to me, told me she wanted to marry me. I said I wasn't interested, and she told me, 'If that's true I'll marry the first person who asks me.' I told her go ahead, it was a free country. The last I heard she was living in Europe."

"According to a recent newspaper article, her

father, a big lumber baron in the Northwest, passed away a few months ago. As his sole heir, she came into millions."

"I wouldn't care if she had all the money in the world. That woman has more than one screw loose."

"Keanu, your father shouldn't have told you this on your wedding day. I hope she won't cause you any problems," his mother said.

"I'll certainly have to tell Lani if Charlene sticks her head on this island. Here comes my beautiful bride now."

"Hi, honey," she said. "Mom wanted to know if you'd like to come down to the pit when the boys take the pigs out. She'd like to begin serving our guests. There must be at least two hundred people here. I didn't know we had that many friends." She laughed. "I know Mom and Dad invited everyone in town. I've seen people I haven't seen in years."

"Well, just shows how popular you are."

The wedding reception went on into the wee hours. Everyone agreed it was not only a beautiful wedding, but a fabulous holiday party as well. When Keanu and Leilani finally could slip away, they spent the night on Beach Road, and caught the first plane out in the morning for Honolulu and then San Francisco.

Leilani discovered the DeYoung Museum had a wood exhibit. It thrilled Keanu to see all the wood carvings from around the world. The young couple walked around the city and visited as many art galleries they could. They spent their honeymoon at the St. Francis in Union Square, making it simple for them to catch the trolley going to North Beach, and the marina.

Several days later they rented a car and began the scenic drive to Carmel. They stopped at every gallery along the way. Christmas Eve found them at the Pine Inn in Carmel sitting around a roaring fire, drinking eggnog and enjoying many unusual dishes the hotel owner and his wife had prepared.

"What's inside this pie crust?" Lani asked.

"It's called a beefsteak and kidney pie," said the proprietor. "Something most people in England love to eat. It's this time of year I miss London so much. Do you like the pie?" she asked.

"I love it. I wonder if I can buy kidneys at home so I can make it for us."

"I hope you can, ipo, this is just so ono. That means good in Hawaiian." Keanu explained to their hosts and the few other guests who were also enjoying the food.

The day after Christmas, Leilani wanted to drive to Big Sur. To her, it ranked as one of the most beautiful spots on the mainland. When they woke up, rain deluged the sidewalk.

"Darling, come back to bed. We don't need to go today. Hopefully the weather will be better tomorrow. I wanted to look at the galleries in Carmel before we went back to the airport. But we can do it today instead of making the wet drive." Leilani tucked her body under the covers, showing only her head.

"No, let's go today, ipo, a little rain won't hurt us."

The weather tried to cooperate for them, the rain stopped for most of their journey. Lani saw a wood carving shop on the side of the road so they made it their first stop. The rain began pelting just as they were exiting the car. They ran to the front door of the gallery and went inside. Keanu was intrigued with the wood carvings on display and studied them intently.

"You like my work?" asked a young man with black hair and a black beard.

"Yes, I do. I carve wood myself."

"I'm John Noble, this is my gallery."

"I'm Keanu Emery, and I'm from the island of Molokai. This is my wife, Leilani. We're on our honeymoon."

"Congratulations. My wife Cathy and I were just married a few months ago."

"Honey, since you like John's work, maybe he'd like to send a few pieces over to our gallery, and we could send him a few of yours. Not the big ones, until we know he likes them, or can sell them."

"I like your idea, Leilani," said John. He kept watching Leilani, trying to flirt with her.

"Don't pay any attention to him, Leilani," said Cathy. "He flirts with everyone."

Not used to such overt flirting, it made Leilani uncomfortable, but she couldn't tell Keanu until they left.

"Keanu, I'm starved. We've driven a long way south and it's time we should make our return trip back to Carmel. You don't want to be driving this road at night."

"Right you are, ipo. Here's our address in Molokai, John. Nice to have met you both."

"Same here," he replied while placing his hand on Leilani's arm. "Leilani, I'm a big tease. I hope I didn't offend you."

Keanu and Leilani got back into their car, and began driving north. Leilani saw a café overlooking the water, so Keanu stopped the car and the two of them went inside. They sat and held hands in front of a huge stone fireplace with a welcoming fire. While the roaring flames warmed them, they watched an angry ocean with waves splashing and thrashing against the rocks and the large plate glass window. Protected from the cold, they felt cozy and comfortable.

"It's beautiful here, but I like Molokai better. Honey, when the waitress comes, would you order me a hamburger and fries please, and share a chocolate malt with me? I want to go wash my hands," said Leilani as she stood up.

"Sure, honey."

When Leilani returned, she told Keanu what she thought of John. "You know what they used to say in high school. Rovin' eyes and roamin' fingers. He may be a wonderful carver, but I'm not sure I like him. Cathy was very nice though."

"It's okay, ipo, you probably won't ever see him again."

Chapter Sixteen

Even on an island as laid back as Molokai, Leilani felt her closeness with Keanu waning, and she didn't know how to cope with it. Two years had passed since their honeymoon on the mainland.

Maybe my pregnancy is the problem. I'm so busy at the gallery.

The gallery Leilani opened a few years previously grew in volume, she sold almost every one of her paintings, and Keanu's wood carvings made a great hit with the tourists.

One afternoon while she was working in the gallery, a pretty blonde haole came through the doorway.

"I love all the carving you have in here," said the stranger. She carefully eyed all the carvings as she perused the store.

"May I help you? Are you visiting on Molokai?" Leilani smiled at her.

"No, I've moved here. My fiancé asked me to, and so I want to furnish the house I'm renting with some typical artifacts of the island."

"Well, please let me know what you would like. If you need furniture, you should probably be buying it on Oahu, and having Young's ship it here. We're pretty isolated for a lot of the niceties."

"I'd like to buy this bowl, looks wonderful for serving salad. Do you have servers to go with it?"

"Yes, of course, here are several to choose from." Leilani placed several sets of salad servers in front of her.

"I'll take these. By the way, my name is Charlene Harper, and I'll be starting a job at the library."

"I'm Leilani Emery. Very nice to meet you."

Charlene gave her a full once-over with her eyes, then smiled. "You're pregnant. When is the baby due?"

"I started showing early. Baby shouldn't be here for another seven months. I'll be glad when I deliver. This tummy bump is a heavy load."

"Could you tell me who carved the bowl I'm buying?"

"My husband, Keanu. I think he does a magnificent job."

Charlene's lips curled in an almost-smile. "Yes, he does." *It will be great when I can parade him around wherever we're living, and tell everyone about my husband, the artisan.* "Thank you, Leilani. See you around sometime."

At dinner that night, Leilani couldn't wait to tell Keanu about the sale she had made that afternoon, and the haole lady who bought it.

"Did she tell you her name?" Keanu asked.

"Charlene Harper. Why do you ask? She

seemed very nice, and I was thinking of inviting her over for dinner. It must be hard not knowing anyone here. Although she did say her fiancé invited her to join him on Molokai."

Keanu's face blanched. "Leilani, come sit down please. We need to have a serious conversation." Keanu waited until his wife poured each of them a cup of coffee and sat down at the side of the kitchen table. "Ipo," he began, "I should have told you much sooner."

"Told me what?"

"When my parents were here for the wedding, they told me Charlene Harper had been running around Bend, telling everyone she was flying to Molokai to marry me. I dated her once or twice, and she proposed to me. I told her no. And her response in return was to tell me she would marry the first person who asked her. The last I heard about her she was living somewhere in Europe, and was unhappy."

"But why all this ruse of saying she was going to marry you?"

"Honey, she's crazy as a three-dollar bill. Besides, Charlene could be dangerous, and I worry about you and our baby."

"But what could she do?"

"Believe me, she's capable of anything. I don't want you fraternizing with her. Please, ipo."

"Of course, I won't, but she told me she was working at the library. You know how often I'm there. And how many times do we meet people we know at the grocery store?"

"Can you have your mom go shopping with you? I truly don't want you walking around alone. I didn't want to tell you but someone has been following me on my bike from school, drives on past from our house once I get off the bike. I know it must be Charlene. She has our home address now."

"You be careful, darling. I just realized the person she is calling her fiancé is you."

"I think we should let George know, too."

"I agree. She knows how to create problems for us. What a mess."

Charlene began her job at the library. She memorized the faces and names of everyone she met. *Can never tell when they might be useful to me.*

Every day, Charlene thought about ways to annoy Keanu and get under his skin. Since he found out she was following him, he would take different routes to and from school.

One Sunday afternoon when the Emerys were at the Coffee Plantation enjoying the music, Charlene approached the table.

"Keanu, how wonderful to see you," she gushed. "And little Leilani, well you're not so little now are you? Do you have a name picked out yet?"

Somewhat flustered by her comments, Leilani didn't answer her. Keanu's looks became cold and unwelcome.

"May I join you?"

"We're just leaving," said Keanu. His words spit icicles. Keanu helped Leilani out of the chair and away from the table.

They walked to their car. After securing Leilani on the passenger side, Keanu climbed into the driver's seat. As he drove down the highway towards Kalae, he realized another car followed them out of the parking lot and onto the highway.

"How could she be following us? We left her sitting at the table."

"It took me awhile to get you comfortably seated. She probably got out and parked outside on the road, waiting for us."

"Is the car still following?"

"Yes, damn it," answered Keanu.

Once they arrived at Malia and Mike's home, Leilani was glad to see other cars in the driveway. "At least she won't be able pull up in the driveway. Where did the car go?"

"It drove on up the road. But I'm sure she'll be back."

Keanu kept a close watch out the window. The car had stopped. The driver drove it down the hill, and then back up. The car made a final turn and left the area. Keanu asked everyone to sit in the living room, so he could tell them what was happening.

"I didn't think she was as crazy as this, but I worry about Lani, especially with the baby's due date not so far off."

Miffed by what had occurred at the Coffee Plantation, Charlene thought about what she could do to annoy Keanu and maybe cause Leilani to lose the baby. *I know where they live. They never lock the doors.*

It was well after midnight when Charlene drove over to Beach Road. She parked the car on a side street, and decided to walk the rest of the way. Aided by the darkness, she snuck into their home and taped a picture of her in a compromising position with Keanu on the refrigerator. Keanu's face had been super-imposed.

When Keanu walked into the kitchen the next

morning, he saw the picture—furious at what Charlene had done, but glad he could take the offensive picture down and dispose of it inside his shirt before Leilani joined him to eat breakfast. Not wanting to upset her any more than she had been, he took the picture to the police station.

"George, something has to be done about Charlene Harper. Can she be charged with breaking and entering?"

"Yes, but it won't keep her away long enough. The judge would probably put her on probation anyway. I'll think of something. Of course, the police department will know to keep an eye on her. Maybe you or Malia could go grocery shopping with Leilani, walk her home when she has worked at the gallery."

"Just another mother-daughter activity," said Malia, after hearing about the kitchen incident. "You probably should tell Leilani, but don't let her see that picture. Knowing my daughter, it could be very upsetting to her."

A few days later, Malia was at the library checking out books. Charlene happened to be the one at the front counter helping her. "You're Malia Palani, aren't you?"

"Yes."

"I saw your wonderful quilts in the Community Center. I wondered if you would teach me how to quilt." She smiled at Malia.

Malia didn't quite know how to answer her. "I'm sorry, I don't have time to give you lessons, but I will find someone to do so." Malia wanted to leave the library as quickly as possible. She saw Paul Kanga come through the door, and walked up to him. "Paul," she whispered, "ask me to have a cup of coffee with you. I've got to get out of here gracefully."

"Malia, how nice to see you. Do you think you might have time to have some coffee with me?"

"I'd love to." She and Paul walked down the library steps together. "You don't have to take me for a coffee. I just wanted to get away from that blonde haole. Bad karma."

Paul looked toward the woman Malia mentioned. A *déjà vu* went through his head. Paul's equilibrium was taxed to the core by the sight of Charlene in the library. *I'll really have to play it cool. She can't recognize me. It's been too many years, and I've added a bit of girth since then.*

Recovering, he spoke to Malia, "I still would like to take you for coffee." He turned away from Charlene. "You can tell me more about the history of Molokai, and also what seems to be the problem."

They sat down at the local coffee hangout, ordered, and reclined back in their chairs.

"That woman, Charlene Harper, has been stalking Keanu ever since she arrived on the island. Today, she asked me to teach her to quilt. I wouldn't go near her with a ten-foot pole let alone do anything to help her. Sorry, Paul, I don't sound very nice. But she has upset Leilani a lot, and you know Leilani is pregnant."

"First, why don't you let me find someone to teach her how to quilt. Betty Sugahara in my congregation does beautiful work, and maybe she would take the time."

"I could hug you, Paul. Thank you so much. That really takes a big load off my shoulders.

That night Paul's sleep was interrupted by dreams from his life as Jack Metzger. A blonde woman had approached him in the bar, happy to accompany him back to his apartment. "I like it rough, Jack." *I'm afraid I could hurt her. But I can give her what she wants.* He grabbed her shoulders in a rough gesture, and took her hard. Her fingernails dug into his back. He anchored his body against her, thrusting up and down till his body expelled all the juice inside of him.

Paul woke, his legs were sticky with semen, and the sheets wet. *I haven't had one of these in a long time.* Paul had to change the sheets, and take a shower before he could crawl back into bed. *It's been so long since I've had a woman, I haven't even thought about it. Charlene was like a tiger. I still can feel the scratches on my back from that night. I must avoid her at all costs. I don't want to say anything to Joe, because he could blurt out something that could ruin my life.*

The next day, Betty arrived at the library and asked to speak to Charlene. When she saw her, her jaw dropped. "My name is Betty Sugahara. You're haole. Pastor Paul didn't tell me that."

Charlene seemed rather taken aback by her comment but she smiled at the lady addressing her. "Won't you teach me to quilt? I'll be happy to pay you."

"I don't want money. When can you meet me at the fabric store?"

"How about tomorrow afternoon after two? That's when I finish at the library."

The next day when Charlene arrived at the appointed time, Betty was already there engaged in conversation with the store clerk.

"This is what you use for your backing," said Betty. Her tone was sharp and condescending. "Now you pick out the fabric you want. You can buy templates of some of the more common motifs. That would save you a lot of time from cutting out patterns."

Betty, a no-nonsense tiny Japanese lady, felt somewhat intimidated by a haole like Charlene. The only haoles she had encountered were during the war years when she and her family were sent off the island to an internment camp.

"I like these little things, they look like baby turtles."

Betty thought to herself: how can a haole be so dumb? "Of course, they're turtles."

"I wanted to make a large spread. This piece you showed me is terribly small."

"Small good for beginner."

Charlene paid no attention to Betty's sharp reply. "What do they call turtles in Hawaiian?"

"They're honu," answered the clerk.

"That's what I want, little yellow and maybe some pale green ones. Oh, I like this fabric," said Charlene pulling out one of yellow cotton with a tiny white flower print. "And this pale green. It's perfect."

"You know the measurements she'll need," Betty said to the clerk. "Give her thread, and needles, and some extra yellow fabric so she can bind the quilt. She'll also need a medium-sized hoop."

Charlene smiled at the clerk. "Hello, I'm Charlene. What's your name?"

"Suki," the clerk said as she smiled back.

"I'll also need some scissors and a tape measure and a ruler. Can we start this afternoon, Betty?"

"No," she replied, not softening her biting words. "Need to fix dinner for my family. How about tomorrow? Where you live?"

"That will be perfect, Betty." Charlene gave her a sweet smile counteracting the harsh words she received from Betty. She gave her the address after Betty said they could meet at ten the following morning.

The next day, Betty arrived promptly and was ushered inside. Her mouth dropped open when she saw a room full of photographs of Keanu Emery and Charlene dancing, kissing on the beach. The pictures stared out into the room. Snapshots were collaged in frames. Betty knew Leilani, and she was shocked by what she saw.

"I see you like my pictures. Keanu Emery and I are getting married, and he is going back to Oregon with me."

"You lolo," Betty whispered to herself. "He's married to Leilani, and they're having a baby soon."

"It doesn't matter. He loves me. It's a simple matter to get a divorce."

Betty didn't want to say any more. She would do what she promised Pastor Paul. Betty sat down at the table where Charlene had put all the materials purchased the day before. She instructed Charlene what to do, and showed her by example. It didn't take long for Charlene to learn. "You sure you don't want sewing machine to do this?"

I can't wait to get out of this house. She knows how to sew, why she needed instruction. Betty shook her head. *I can't wait to leave and see Pastor Paul. Something isn't right, and he should know.*

"I think you understand how to do this now. "If you have problems, go see Suki, and she will get in touch with me."

"Thank you for all your help, Betty," said Charlene as she walked her to the front door. "Have a nice day. Mahalo. Aloha."

Charlene put her back against the door frame

after she closed the door.

She's such a simpleton. I'll make this quilt, and fix it especially for Leilani. I'll get her out of the way if it's the last thing I do. She made an evil laugh.

Charlene worked on her honu quilt every day until she completed it. *Too bad it can't be salvaged from what I have in mind.* A quick trip to the grocery store yielded the supplies she needed. Taking an empty jar from a kitchen shelf, she filled it with a combination of ketchup and tomato juice till it reached the desired consistency she was looking for.

She carried her finished quilt into the kitchen and placed it in the sink. Charlene shook the jar, opened it and poured the contents onto the quilt. "That should do it," she laughed. "I've got this nice box and tissue to wrap it in. I'll fold it so the red doesn't show. Then tonight, I'll set it on their front doorstep. What a surprise they'll have in the morning." Her voice was almost sing-song. *I hope this scares Leilani enough she could lose the baby. I don't want Keanu to have any familial ties here. Keanu belongs to me, and I mean to have him.* She closed and wrapped the box with beautiful yellow and white ribbon. "I can't wait until midnight tonight."

The hours seem to pass slowly. Charlene went out for a burger, took a purposeful walk along Ala Malama, looking into all the store windows. Looking at her watch, she shook her head. *The time is passing too slowly. Guess I'll go back home and read until the appointed hour.*

It was after midnight when Charlene took the wrapped box, put it in the passenger seat of her car and made a surreptitious trip to Beach Road. She turned the car lights off, so no one could see her driving. She drove to the end of the street, turned around and parked the car a few doors from Keanu and Leilani's home, leaving the motor running. With the silence of a cat she walked up to the front door and set the package down. Charlene held her breath as she walked back to her car, climbed in the driver's seat and drove to the end of the block before she put the car lights on. She couldn't wait for the morning to arrive.

Keanu walked to the front door in the morning, getting ready to leave for school when he saw the attractive box sitting there. He returned to the kitchen with the box in tow and set it on the table. "Looks like someone left us a present. Do you want to open it, ipo?"

Leilani took off the pretty yellow ribbon, and opened the box, revealing something wrapped in tissue. She took the quilt out of the box. "It's so pretty. Oh, my God," she screamed. "It's covered in blood."

Keanu ran to her side and took one look at what Leilani had dropped onto the table. "You know this has to be Charlene. We can prove it. We've got to let the police handle this. She needs a restraining order or something worse. Are you all right, ipo? Call your mom and have her take you to see Kimo to make certain."

"Yes, honey," Leilani whispered. She had been shaken by the turn of events. "Can't George get her off the island somehow?"

Chapter Seventeen

It was a Friday afternoon after school when Keanu went to pick up the mail at the post office. An unfamiliar handwriting greeted him as he opened the letter. *Well, I'll be damned. It's from John Noble, asking if he and his wife would be welcome for a visit. I have my nemesis around here, and now Lani will have hers.*

Keanu gathered the rest of the mail from their postbox, stuffed it inside his shirt, hopped on his bicycle, and rode home. He couldn't wait to tell Lani the latest news.

"Honey, we have a request for some visitors. Can we put them up in your apartment?"

"I don't see why not. Who's coming?"

"Well, I have to write back and tell them it's okay. It's John Noble and his wife, Cathy."

"I thought we'd never have to see them again. I can't believe they actually took us up on your offer. We'll make the best of it. Find out when they want to come, and let's tell a small lie. If they want to come for a week, tell them fine, but we have company coming the day after John says they want to leave. That way we won't have to continually entertain them."

"You're being such a good sport, ipo, pregnant and all." Keanu gave her a kiss and hugged her.

"While they're here, maybe we could plan a joint art show with his and your pieces at the gallery."

"Wonderful idea." Keanu gave Leilani another big hug.

"And maybe we could get a couple of good quilters to show their work also. I'll ask Mom to make some suggestions. I'd love to display a quilt or two of hers," Leilani said.

John wrote back he and Cathy were delighted they could be guests. "One week would be wonderful. Can we come in November? Say around the first week? I'd like to bring several of my pieces. I know they would display well in your store. I'll take a large crate filled with your carvings back with me. See you in a few months. I'll keep you posted on our arrival. Could you see about a car rental for us?"

Leilani would already have delivered their child, so they knew she would be feeling a lot better after losing the baby weight.

"Keanu, what will we do if Charlene is still here then? Of course, she'll come to the store for the reception. There's no way we can't invite her, since we will have a notice on the window, and also on the bulletin board at the market."

"Don't worry your pretty head about her coming. She may have gone back to Oregon by then. Let's just concentrate on having a beautiful, healthy baby."

A few months later, Malia and Leilani were downtown. It was very close to her due date, and Malia was taking her to see Kimo at the clinic. They had just arrived in his waiting room when Leilani felt a whoosh of water and saw a puddle on the floor.

"Mom, my water broke. Get Kimo. What do I do?"

"We don't have time to take you to the hospital."

Kimo's nurse realized what was happening and rushed over to Leilani.

"I'm going to put you into one of the rooms, and Kimo will be here directly. How often are you having contractions?"

"About two minutes apart, I think. They were further apart before. The last two I'm certain were even two minutes."

"I've got to prep you as much as I can, if you aren't completely dilated already. Malia, please help Leilani undress and put this gown on, and then into bed. I'll be right back," she said as she ran out of the room to retrieve her razor, soap, and water.

"Kimo, you're going deliver my grandchild. It's good to see you finally got here. I was worried I'd have to deliver the baby myself." Malia laughed as she threw a kiss to her son.

Kimo felt Leilani's stomach. "Nurse, nurse, Pili. There's no time to prep. This baby is pushing to greet the world."

"Oh, God, it hurts." Leilani let out a loud scream of pain.

"I know, honey, but your baby will be here very soon." Kimo reassured her, as he made preparations for the baby's birth. "Mom, call Keanu. He'll want to be here, too. Pili, get a washcloth and wipe Leilani's forehead. Now push again, hard, Leilani."

With the last push, the head crowned, and Kimo held up a baby girl. He took the surgical scissors and removed the umbilical cord, tying one end at the baby's navel. Pili took the baby over to the surgical sink and gave her a careful washing. She wrapped the vocal young lady in blankets and gently placed her in Leilani's arms. Pili changed all the linens on the bed, and dressed Leilani in a clean hospital gown. Leilani snuggled her newborn baby against her breast and within moments, the baby fell asleep.

"Isn't she beautiful? Keanu and I already picked out a name. It's Malia Rose after both our mothers. She will be called Lia."

At that moment Keanu walked through the door of the hospital room with nearly more packages than he could carry. "Where's my little girl? Can I hold her? She's so beautiful, just like her mother." He leaned over to kiss Leilani. Keanu also handed the new mother a pink stuffed animal. "I thought this would be fun for her to cuddle. It's so soft." Keanu was filled with love for his new baby.

"What an adorable bear. I know Lia will make it her favorite. When can I go home, Kimo?"

Kimo had remained in the room with the happy family. "I'd like to keep you overnight to make certain there are no complications. Your delivery was easy..."

Leilani interrupted him. "What do you mean easy? It was painful as hell."

"Compared to other births, dear sister, Lia arrived without any problem whatsoever. My niece will be the healthiest baby on the island if I have anything to say about it." Everyone laughed at his comments.

Chapter Eighteen

"How much property comes with this house?" Charlene questioned Tom Millard, a real estate agent who brought her to see a house he had just listed.

"Do you see that little gray-blue cottage?"

"Yes."

"Your property would be about fifty feet from the side of that house to the beginning of this place. It's very private out here. Your neighbor is Joe Obregon. He's a fisherman. He's also not well, I'm told. The rumor around town is that he has Parkinson's. Joe was a hell-raiser and heavy drinker until about five years ago. Sober as a judge now. He's become a nice guy. You've probably seen him selling fish on Ala Malama."

"Oh, I have. I've even bought fish from him." Charlene was clinging to every word. She'd heard other gossip too. Joe was once married to Malia Palani. *I wonder if Leilani is his daughter. I'll have to find out more. I haven't seen him with any of the family. Could be bad blood.*

"Do you think you'd like to buy this place? Owners are anxious to sell because they've moved to Maui to care for some family members."

Charlene paced up and down the property line before she gave him her answer. "I'd love this place. Look at the ocean, well I guess it's the channel, but it's beautiful."

"The furniture comes with it," the realtor added. "It's available for occupancy on a very short escrow."

Charlene walked through the house. It had a modest kitchen, two modern bathrooms, and two large bedrooms, as well as a living room, dining room, and spacious lanai. "I'll take it, and I'd like to move in as soon as possible." She smiled as she told Tom her decision.

At the tiny grocery market across the highway from her driveway, she posted a note for a housekeeper, and in no time, Nali, a young Samoan girl, applied and was hired. Charlene expected a clean house by the time she moved in.

Meanwhile, Tom contacted George Kapule and told him what had transpired in his dealings with Charlene Harper.

"Having her on the other side of the island is a big help in keeping her away from the Emerys. I just hope she will stay east end, or go off the island for good." George said. He would be happy to relay that news to the older and younger Palanis.

"Can you restrict her movements?" Tom asked.

"No more than telling her to stay away from the Emerys. She's been told not to talk to them or harass them in any way. Keanu already had a restraining order placed on her. I'm pleased to know she's moving out of Kaunakakai. What house did she buy?"

Tom replied. "She bought the Sweeney place next to Joe Obregon."

"I hope she doesn't get any bright ideas with him. He's not well and can't drink. Charlene has been known to put away a few."

Once the owners and Charlene agreed upon the price, a deal was made, and a few days later, Charlene met the sellers at the bank in Kaunakakai and paid cash for her new place to live. Nali was thrilled to be her housekeeper. Not caring to remember her name, she told Nali, "I'm calling you Sally. That better be all right with you, young lady."

An affirmative nod was the answer. Sally made about five of Charlene, and she was as strong as an ox. Even-tempered and quiet, she had three basic words of speech in her vocabulary: yes, no, and thank you.

When Charlene moved in a few days later, the house had been scrubbed shiny clean. Charlene hired a truck and two strapping young men to move all her belongings from her rental in town. Charlene planned to purchase a station wagon equipped with all the latest gadgets, the main one being four-wheel drive. This would give her good wheels to go exploring. It would become her preferred pastime because it would allow her to discover more about the Palanis.

Charlene became familiar with Joe's routine, although the closest encounter they had was a smile and a wave. Deciding to do something about it, she baked a batch of chocolate chip cookies, and when she saw Joe's truck in his driveway, she placed the cookies on a plate and deposited herself at his front door.

"Hello, I'm your new neighbor. I thought you might like some cookies." Charlene tried to look inside

Joe's home while handing him the dish.

"Like to come in? You can share the cookies with me."

Charlene gave him a big smile as she entered the front room. "I like all your furniture. I absolutely adore Molokai," Charlene gushed. "How long have you lived here?"

"In this house or on Molokai?" Joe asked her.

"Well, both, if you want to tell me. Are we going to eat the cookies standing, or may I sit down?"

"'Scuse my manners. C'mon into the kitchen. We can sit at the table there." Joe chuckled as he led the way to his tiny kitchen. "You can have your choice of tea, coffee, or I may have some POG in the fridge."

"Water will be just fine."

Joe managed to bring two glasses of water to the table. "I'm not as mobile as I used to be. Doc says I have Parkinson's. It's nice to have a neighbor. My name is Joe."

"I'm Charlene." She gave him another warm smile. "Maybe you'll come over some evening and have dinner with me. It seems pretty darn quiet on this side of the island."

"Molokai is always quiet. But this place will always be in my blood, started the first day I arrived here."

"Now you've really got me intrigued. Please tell me your story. I'd love to hear it." Charlene said, as she helped herself to a cookie on the plate. Eager to hear what light Joe could shed on the Palani family, she encouraged him to speak.

"When I first came to Molokai, it wasn't by choice. I served as cabin boy aboard a beautiful private yacht owned by a wealthy family from Lisbon. I don't know if you know I came from Portugal."

"No, I didn't."

"Well anyway, we were in a horrific storm. It battered and bashed the yacht until it sunk. I was the only survivor; a cargo boat rescued me from a plank I was clinging to. I should have landed in Honolulu. But the rescue boat had also borne the brunt of the storm, and we limped into the closest port which was Kaunakakai. A group of Hawaiian men and women met us as we walked towards town, or what could be called a town. Among the group came a beautiful young woman with shiny black hair hanging down almost to her waist." Joe sat back in his chair and closed his eyes. He could see and remember the exact time and place. "She placed a lei over my head and said some words to me. Since I didn't know any English, I had no idea what she said, but she was beautiful, and I fell head over heels for her. She's now Malia Palani."

"Malia, the one who did the quilt show, yes?"

"Yes. Her parents invited everyone from our boat to a luau to celebrate our safety and welcome us to Molokai. The welcoming committee held the luau in the Coconut Grove. Malia sat next to me. She showed me how to open a coconut, and each time she taught me a word of English. I followed her around like a puppy dog every time I saw her. It would be many months before the cargo ship would be repaired and sail back to Portugal, after delivering our cargo to Honolulu. She was only fourteen, several years younger than me, but we knew we were in love. We wanted to get married, but her father insisted we wait until she graduated from high school. Malia was very unhappy with his decision, but she obeyed. I told her I would be back for her."

"And you returned. Of course, you returned. When?"

"A month after Malia graduated, I came back to Kaunakakai. We had written letters to each other, each time my English improved, as well as her writing and reading of English. She didn't like school. She told me that in every one of her letters. We married in the Grove a few months after I returned. Her brothers built us a hale, and we lived there 'til December 10, 1941. Malia was pregnant, and we were over the moon with joy. But the Japanese bombed Pearl. Mike Palani, Kimo Pascua, and I decided to canoe to Honolulu to see what we could do to help with the war effort."

"I know Mike Palani is here, but where is Kimo?"

"He never made it home, killed in one of the battles on Guadalcanal."

"I'm sorry. A lot of your friends must have died during the war."

Joe's voice softened. "Too many of them."

"Where was Malia all this time?"

"She remained in Kaunakakai. As soon as the war was over, she joined me in San Diego. I liked the Navy life and continued re-upping. Over the next few years we had two more children."

"But it sounds like you were a happy family," said Charlene.

Joe took a long drink of water and stared into space. Then he spoke. "I was the most stupid man in the world. I liked the sailor's life and the reputation. I began drinking a lot, going into bars, and seeking the high life with flashy ladies I met there. I hated to go home to what I called a dull wife and noisy children. Malia wanted a simpler life. I belittled her, and abused her verbally. She disliked the people I hung around with. She had every right to be angry with me, but she would just smile and say, 'yes, Joe.' One day, I signed on for a ship going to the Med. I literally left her sitting at the dinner table in San Diego, stranded with three kids. I had her served with divorce papers by mail later. Today, I wouldn't argue with anyone about my stupid choices, or what an awful person I'd become. I gave up so much to be that macho sailor, and now I have so little. I've been more than mean to her, and Mike hates my guts. I hate his for marrying Malia."

"Why did you return to Molokai then?"

"I had nowhere else to go. I had no family left in Portugal, the friends I made at an early age scattered to the four winds. I mustered out of the Navy, feeling too old to stay on active duty. I wanted more freedom. On Molokai, I knew I could fish and, with my Navy pension, I'd have enough money to live on. It's pretty easy to live off the land here. I've been back five years now."

"Gossip around the island says that Malia has a restraining order against you. I can't believe that's true."

"Believe it. I saw Malia in front of the bakery, first time when I thought I was sober. Asked her to have a cup of coffee with me, told her I wanted her back, and when she said no, I became so enraged I grabbed her arm and yelled at her. Guess I'd had a bit too much to drink. It wasn't a good scene. I was mean as hell. Good old belligerent Joe. I will regret it 'til the day I die. But it's water under the bridge now. Hopefully with Paul's help, I can make amends."

"Paul Kanga?" asked Charlene.

"Yes, he and I served on the same ship in the

Med. He left the Navy to go to a Bible college or something like that. I hadn't seen him in years when he showed up at the gunwale of my boat."

"That's some story, Joe Obregon. I just want you to know, I'll be your friend, too."

Charlene patted his arm as she stood up. "I've got to do some errands now. Hope we can have another visit soon. By the way, I'm a good cook." *Ply him with good food. That'll help.* "See you later."

She waved as she walked down the path over to her house. *What a stroke of luck, maybe I can enlist Joe in my plan to get Keanu. He doesn't love the Palanis. He didn't talk about his children. Probably doesn't know them either.*

A few days later Charlene noticed a very tired neighbor going inside his house. She walked over and knocked on the door. Joe partially opened it.

"Joe, I made a nice roast for myself today. Would you let me bring you a piece plus a baked potato?"

"If I said no, I'd be an idiot. I'm so tired, Charlene, it's difficult to stand."

"Leave your door open, I'll be back in a flash with your dinner. I'll put it on the kitchen table. You don't even need to talk to me. I can see how tired you are."

Very grateful for the hot meal, the next time Joe saw Charlene he asked her if she would like to go fishing with him on the Folly.

"Sounds like great fun, Joe." Charlene reciprocated by preparing dinner, a platter of fried fish from their catch that day, green salad accompanied by Hawaiian bread, and some sliced mangoes. Since Joe was no longer drinking hard liquor, he sat at the kitchen table nursing a glass of iced tea from the pitcher Charlene had prepared for the two of them.

"It smells wonderful, Charlene. It's very kind of you to do this for me."

"Not a problem, Joe, and besides there are some questions I'd like to ask you. Something has been bothering me for a long time." Charlene plated the two dishes for them when she sat at the table across from Joe.

Joe wondered what kind of questions Charlene might ask since he knew about the Keanu connection. Paul had managed to keep him up to date on the Charlene saga, so he had been forewarned about her aberrant behavior.

"Joe, just how well do you know Paul Kanga?"

Joe, surprised by her question, answered immediately. "Since we met in the Med serving on the same ship."

"It's funny you didn't meet on Molokai before. I heard he went from Molokai to the Med."

"I was transferred from San Diego. And while Paul did Navy duty in Molokai the same time I lived here, our paths would never have crossed. Malia and I didn't have anything to do with any military, complete separation. I doubt Malia's father would even have allowed us to speak to them. The natives and the military didn't associate with each other. I don't even remember if Paul ever told me where he served before the Med. I was in the Pacific during the war."

"Has he ever lived in Singapore?"

"I don't think so. Why?" Joe was on his guard now.

"He looks like the spitting image of a man I once knew several years ago. His name was Jack Metzger. He dealt drugs, had a big falling out with some of the other dealers, and a contract was put out on his head. He disappeared into thin air. Then I meet this Paul Kanga. I can't believe two men look so much alike. Even the mannerisms are the same."

Joe listened carefully, trying not to show any expression on his face. He knew that if Charlene knew, there's going to be hell to pay, what with Charlene's penchant for making trouble. "Well, Paul Kanga is the only name I've known him by. What surprised me is that he became a preacher. Isn't it said that everyone has a double?"

"I'm having a new toy shipped from Honolulu." Charlene was quick to change the subject.

"Toy?"

"An adult toy," Charlene smiled. "A lovely woody station wagon with four-wheel drive is being shipped from Honolulu. I want to not only read about secret places but explore the island. Maybe you could show me sights I couldn't see, yet alone get to, except by four-wheel drive."

"My pleasure," said Joe. "Get me out in the air and not talking to myself. I can at least ride even if I don't have strength to fish."

A few months had passed. Charlene enjoyed fishing on the Folly, and Joe had taken her to several hidden heiaus on the island. "Joe, I'm still shuddering from the fact the place we went to today was used for human sacrifices."

Joe laughed. "Charlene. That was a long time ago. By any chance do you want to have some target practice? We could go hunting for deer. It's hard for me to get around by myself for an activity like that. Anyway, it's not a human sacrifice, and I love venison."

Charlene couldn't help but smile to herself.

Of course, I know how to shoot a high-powered rifle. Maybe I can shoot Leilani, just by accident. She wanted to laugh aloud, but restrained herself. "I'm no sharpshooter, but I can probably hit a deer. If it's a big enough target," she added. "That should be a fun outing."

"How about going next Sunday morning? Can you be ready by seven?"

"I'll be in your driveway with my wagon. Do you have another rifle?"

"Yes. And I'll be glad to lend it to you."

"I'll bring a lunch, if that's okay with you."

"Usually I end up with a jar of peanut butter. A real lunch would be great. Thank you."

"See you Sunday morning."

Charlene arrived at the appointed hour wearing fatigue camos and a hat to match. She prepared a lunch of roast beef sandwiches, and several cans of soft drinks. She also tossed in two small camp chairs, knowing they might be in one spot for the duration of the hunt

Joe had her drive to the same spot he had taken Paul to hunt. With difficulty he left the wagon, opened the gate, waited for Charlene to pass through, closing the gate behind them. "Charlene, we're walking over to those kiave trees," Joe said as he sat back in the car. "It's several hundred yards from here. I don't think I can carry everything myself."

"Don't worry about it, Joe. I'll make a second trip. Let's just get you settled where you want to be."

Joe maneuvered out of the woody again, had Charlene hand him the two rifles and the box of shells. When Charlene exited the wagon, she grabbed the two chairs, their lunch and the two of them walked over to the spot Joe had previously indicated.

"Charlene, I haven't been hunting in over a year. I can't go by myself, and Paul has been so busy with his congregation, he hasn't been able to accompany me. Thank you for giving me this special day."

"You know, Paul looks so familiar to me. I just can't get over it. I told you before he's the spitting image of someone I knew in Singapore."

"Really? He told me the last place he served a church was in Palau. I don't know if he's ever been to Singapore." Joe's words were spoken with care not to say anything that could cause his friend problems. He had heard the town gossip concerning Charlene, and he wasn't about to cause his best friend any trouble.

They sat quietly in the kiave grove. Joe looked over at Charlene. He knew she was thinking hard. He could picture the wheels going around in her head. *She's already caused enough trauma on the island. I won't be the one to add to it.*

"Look," he whispered. "Two bucks walking across the field. We need to have them closer before we can take a shot."

Charlene's adrenalin was pumping. To shoot a large animal would be incredible. *I'll have to have my Dad's rifle with the power scope shipped to me. Then a little practice sharp-shooting, and I'll be ready. My plans will be altered a little. But the result will be the same. I'll get Keanu, and maybe eliminate Leilani and the baby. Charlene, you're so clever.* She mentally patted herself on the back.

Joe and Charlene both stood. "Let's aim for the one on the right."

Okay boss," Charlene whispered back. "We both need to shoot at the same time, don't we?"

Joe nodded yes, as he loaded his rifle, ready to

take aim. Within the next few minutes, their buck was bagged. "Charlene, you'll need to drive the wagon over to where we shot the deer. We can load the rest of our gear back in the wagon after we get his carcass inside. He looks like a very heavy fella. I've the strength to lift him, but not carry our prize."

Charlene was back in minutes. She let down the back door of the wagon right next to the buck. The two of them lifted their quarry and Charlene pulled it up so the door would close. She loaded the chairs and remains of their lunch in with the deer. She turned on the motor, and the two of them left the area. Joe opened and closed the gate again, and got back into the station wagon.

"This was a very exciting day for me, to say the least. What's next?"

"We'll go to Misaki's and they'll hang the carcass for a week so all the blood will drain out. Then I'll show you how to skin it, and how to cure the skin if you would like."

"That would be fantastic. What will we do with all the meat? Can you sell it to the grocery store? Do you want to give it away? Shall we have a venison barbecue?"

"Well my freezer can hold a lot, and venison hamburgers are delicious. So are the steaks. We can have our own barbecue. I'd like to invite Paul. Do you have someone you'd like to invite?"

Charlene stared at Joe. Her whole demeanor changed. If anyone had asked him, her eyes looked wild. "No, at least no one who would accept my invitation."

Joe didn't reply.

Chapter Nineteen

On one of Charlene's off-island jaunts to Honolulu, she discovered a jewelry store she really liked. As she admired a beautiful gold bracelet, she noticed an elegantly dressed man setting out loose diamonds and emeralds in a secluded corner. It seemed the store owner wanted to make certain the two of them weren't disturbed. Charlene wasn't to be daunted as she listened closely to whatever bits of conversation she could overhear.

"What do you think?"

"Beautiful, it will take some skill to sell them."

"That's why I came to you, Mr. Leung. You have the reputation for your client's privacy."

"It is my business to be discreet."

"You can see all the stones have been disassembled from their original state. How much can I get for them?"

"I'm certain, a couple of million. But I can't

pay you that. Maybe we can work some kind of deal. Each time a gem is sold you will get a percentage."

"But how do I know I can trust you?"

"You don't. But how do you know I can trust you?" the owner said.

"I want a million dollars up front as insurance," the silver haired man said.

Charlene looked at the man and thought he looked like a silver fox. She told the clerk who was helping her she wanted to buy the bracelet. "Would you happen to have any fine pearl necklaces? Not the everyday kind."

The silver fox overheard her comment, and turned in her direction. Charlene looked at him and gave him a big smile. Then she looked at him again. "I know you from somewhere."

"That's a good pick-up line, young lady. But I think I know you, too. You're Charlene Harper, and you used to live in Singapore."

Charlene looked at the man again. "Oh, my God, I haven't seen you in maybe fifteen years. Your hair is silver now. It used to be coal black. You're ... you're Frank." She paused. "Frank Soriano. What are you doing in Honolulu?"

"A little business with my friend here. Do you have time to have a drink with me?"

"I'd love to, but I want to buy my bracelet first."

Frank spoke to the person he had been dealing with. "Let me buy the bracelet for this lovely young lady." He pulled out several one hundred bills and handed them to the man. "I think this should cover it."

"Frank, that is so generous of you. You don't have to do this. But thank you, thank you." Charlene gushed her words.

"How about the bar at the Halekelani?"

"I love that place. That's where I'm staying."

"What a coincidence. So am I."

The two of them sat in the bar drinking specialty Mai Tais. Even though Charlene could hold her liquor well, the two of them were becoming very familiar with each other. Frank had his hand under a fold in her dress, and would every so often give her a soft kiss, which Charlene returned.

"Why don't we get some dinner?"

"That's a great idea. I'm so hungry. I love the lobster here."

"Charlene, I'd like to talk to you about something in private, away from any prying eyes or ears. Would you mind if we had dinner in my suite? We can order the lobster served there. How about some champagne to go with it?"

"Sounds absolutely wonderful." Charlene was purring. *Maybe I'll get a little sex besides. There's certainly no one on Molokai.*

Charlene looked at Frank, trying to decide the age difference between them. She thought he was about twenty years her senior. She studied his body under his fine beige linen suit, and knew he kept himself fit. She remembered the last time they were together in Singapore. She melted at the thought of his stamina.

When they reached Frank's suite and were inside, he removed his jacket and pulled her close to him. Then he grabbed Charlene's hair. "Why did you leave Singapore you little minx?"

"Oh, Frank, I had things to take care of in Oregon. My parents died in a plane crash. There was so much to do. I was beside myself. I couldn't think. Will you forgive me?" Charlene managed to bring a few tears to her eyes. "After dealing with everything for my parents, I had no desire to return to Singapore. I've been living in Molokai for the last few years."

"You were my only connection to Jack Metzger. When one of my biggest drug deals went south, he disappeared off the face of the earth. My boys spent a couple of years trying to find him and then we just gave up, but I'd kill him myself if I ever saw him again."

"Strange you should mention that. There's a man on Molokai, a minister, who is the spitting image of Jack—same mannerisms, same build—everything. I confronted him, and he denied ever being in Singapore. Said he came from Palau. I live next door to a friend of his, and he tells me the same story. So, I guess I'm wrong."

"One of these days I'll come to Molokai and see for myself. How did you happen to choose Molokai? That's an island I've never seen. I've heard about the leper colony."

"That's far removed from the other parts of the island. You can get there by mule, on horseback or an airplane. I've never had the desire to go."

Frank picked up the hotel phone and asked for room service. "Yes, lobsters for two, a good fruit platter, and your best Champagne, two bottles please. How long will that take?" Once hearing the voice answer on the other side of the phone, he put the phone back in its cradle. "Come here, you."

Charlene walked over to Frank. He wrapped his arms around her and gave her a kiss, his tongue reaching far inside her mouth. He began removing her dress, and threw it on a chair. Charlene unbuttoned Frank's shirt so he could take it off, also. Once they were both naked, he picked up Charlene and carried her to the punai at the far wall of the living room.

"God, Charlene. I want to eat every piece of your body." Frank's tongue began kissing her neck and then her breasts. He laid her down, and lay beside her, all the while, his tongue searched out her body. "I see you keep yourself like the French ladies. I like that." His tongue was insatiable as it found her most inner parts inside her thighs.

Charlene writhed on the punai. "You feel so good, oh, God, you feel marvelous." His tongue moved back and forth sending Charlene into absolute ecstasy. Charlene clasped her fingers around his shaft, which was completely engorged. She wanted to reciprocate with her tongue, but Frank was ready to enter her. His thrusts inside her body inflamed her. Their bodies moved in unison until Frank's arms squeezed Charlene tightly as he came. They both were shaking at the volcanic feeling and lay spent.

Frank put his elbow on the punai, and his hand on his chin. Looking at Charlene, he said, "I really do think we need something to eat to get back some energy." He laughed.

Charlene smiled in agreement. "Do you have more than one beach robe here? I do need to put something on. When is the food coming?"

"Should be here momentarily." The room doorbell rang. "See what I told you."

As they were drinking their champagne, Frank put his glass down and looked at her. "How long were you planning to stay in Honolulu?"

"Probably about a week, shopping, eating at

the restaurants."

"Move all your things in here with me. I'll make it worth your while."

"You already have, Frank. And I'll be happy to stay here. I'm just a couple of doors down the hallway."

The next morning Frank and Charlene sat at a table overlooking Waikiki Beach, drinking mimosas.

"Charlene, I have a business proposition for you."

"I'm listening."

"Every few months, I accumulate some lovely gems that I sell through the owner of the jewelry store where we met. I would like to be able to mail the loose stones from Singapore to you, and let you deliver them to Mr. Leung. It's a lot easier than making a flight here each time. I'd pay you well. What do you think?"

"I believe I could do that for you. I don't have a physical address in Honolulu. In Kaunakakai, people might wonder about boxes coming from Singapore. You certainly wouldn't want your goods left at a front desk of a hotel."

"I thought we might get a post box in Honolulu that would hold different-sized packages. I don't want them all to be the same size."

"That's a good idea."

Charlene, my young friend, you are going to be my patsy if ever anything goes wrong.

"We'll go this afternoon. But first I intend to ravish your body again."

Charlene smiled. She seductively removed the robe she wore. With nothing underneath, she sidled her body next to Frank. He led her back into the king-sized bed they had shared the night before.

"Now, I know all that I missed about you," Charlene said, her legs wrapped around Frank's hips.

After a joint shower, they dressed and took a taxi to the post office. Frank asked Charlene to take out the post box in her name. Frank paid for it by cash. *That should keep me from any mail fraud. Charlene can take the blame. Everything is in her name.*

"Charlene, if I send you clothes from Singapore, will you wear them?"

"Of course, but you don't know my size or anything about my style."

"Your style I know, but just to be on the safe side lets go shopping this afternoon. I'll buy you some clothes."

"I can buy my own clothes, Frank. But thank you."

"No Charlene, this is my gift to you. You have given me a fabulous time this week, and you have helped me solve a thorny business problem."

"Well, then, thank you very much. Can we begin with lunch at the Royal Hawaiian?"

"A fine idea."

After a lunch of Mai Tais and pupus, the two of them walked into all the boutiques along Kalakaua Avenue the main thoroughfare of the city. Charlene tried on several items of clothing.

"I like that white slack outfit on you. There's a nice hat in the window. Try that on, too."

Charlene protested. She shook her head no. "Frank, I can't wear that in Molokai. But, I can wear those cami clothes. That skirt is cute. And so is the matching blouse and jacket."

"There's a pair of slacks that can go with the outfit, also," said the salesgirl.

"Good we'll take those, too. Please total up the white outfit, the cami outfit, and give her the hat, too," said Frank, again pulling out a wad of $100 bills. "She'll find a place to wear it."

Once they left the apparel store, Charlene spied a store window displaying shoes and handbags. It didn't take her long to find what she wanted. Twenty minutes later, with Frank's pocket substantially lighter, they left the store. Their arms loaded with packages, Frank hailed a taxi to take them back to the hotel.

"Charlene, remember when the packages come to the Honolulu box don't open them. Take a taxi to deliver them to Mr. Leung."

"How will I know when to go to the box in Honolulu?"

"I will send you a large box from Singapore. It will come from a store with a note from me."

"I'll remember, Frank. Thank you for all the beautiful clothes and accessories."

By the time the week had passed, Charlene felt sated by all the sex with him. Though she acted sad Frank was returning to Singapore, she was happy to see him go. She had another friend she wanted to see before she returned to Molokai. He had good weed to smoke, and she craved a little of that before she took her flight to Hoolehua.

Like clockwork, Charlene made her regular trip to pick up her mail at the post office. She looked for her first box from Singapore. That would signal it would be time to make another trip to Honolulu, pick up the small parcels and deliver them to Mr. Leung. One afternoon she picked up her mail and signed for a large box with a store label attached. She couldn't wait to get back to the privacy of her home so she could look at the contents. *Can't do this in public. I'll take the box home, look and then come back to do my grocery shopping.*

Charlene pulled into her driveway, took her mail and her box, and hurried inside her home. She plopped down on her new Hawaiian floral print couch and tore the wrapping off her package. With a mighty pull, she lifted off the box cover. *My God, oh, my God, look what that man did. These are gorgeous.* Charlene pulled out several lacy brassieres and matching thongs. The colors were yummy: ecru, coffee, two shades of blue, pale green, and black. These are obviously from Paris. She also found a note amid all the lingerie.

Charlene realized how involved she had become in Frank's business. She delivered all the stones he sent via the Honolulu post box. She began to think about the origin of the stones after reading about several large robberies in Asia and Europe.

I need to separate myself from Frank and everything I'm doing for him. I certainly don't need the money. Even with his suave manners and impeccable wardrobe, I know he's a gangster. I'm sure of it and a tough one with many goons to do his bidding.

She had been involved in Frank's scheme couriering for about six months when she woke up with a start in the middle of the night. *Oh, my God. I've been doing all these things for Frank. I know those jewels are stolen. I've actually been the fence for them. If Frank were ever caught, I'd be the one taking the blame. I need to get out of this mess and soon. I'll go talk to Joe. He's really my only friend here on the island. I just want Frank off my back, and I don't want to go to jail for what I've been doing. I'm an idiot. Big time. I'll ask Joe. He's always wanting to help me.*

Charlene went across the yard to Joe's front door knocked on it, called out, and opened it. Hi, Joe, it's me. Do you have time to talk? I need to discuss something very serious with you," Charlene said when Joe walked out of the kitchen to meet her.

"Come on in, Charlene. Your face looks distressed. You must have a problem. What can I do to help you?"

They sat down at the kitchen table. Joe poured two glasses of iced tea and then sat across from her. "Okay, Charlene, shoot."

"You know how I've been taking trips every couple of weeks to Honolulu?"

"Yes. I was envious of you getting off the island. I would like to do something like that, too."

"You don't want to have been doing what I have been. I've been delivering stolen gems to a jeweler. He melts down the gold, and puts the stones in different settings. I've been doing this for a quasi-friend who lives in Singapore. He's a very powerful man, and if I cross him, he would probably have someone kill me as easy as he finds lighting a cigarette."

"Charlene, you're too smart to be involved in something so illegal. I won't ask how it happened. Let's go talk with George Kapule. He's been on the police force for a long time, and should know what to do."

"He doesn't like me. He might arrest me."

"Worse things could happen to you."

"I know. I know. Can we go now before I lose my courage?"

"Sure, do you want to come in my truck?"

"Lead the way."

Forty minutes later, the two of them were sitting in George's office. He closed the door and comfortably sat in his desk chair.

"Charlene, I appreciate you coming to see me with this information. You're being very forthright and repentant. I'm sure a judge would be lenient on you since you have given me the fodder to help put Frank Soriano in prison for a long time. He's been on a wanted list all over the world but he never seems to surface. I will alert Hawaii 5-0 to all that you've told me. Once we have both men in custody, a court date will be set. Mr. Leung will be prosecuted for his part in fencing and reselling stolen goods. When do you make your next trip to Honolulu? Do you have any way in which to contact Soriano?"

"I'm not sure. Sometimes he arrives with a package, and sometimes he mails it to a post office box in my name. He mails a package to me in Kaunakakai when he wants me to go to Honolulu. It's never the same address, just a clothing store somewhere in Singapore."

"He's a clever bastard. Making you take out the post office box, plying you with lovely clothes and jewelry. He's been using you and using you. You're the one who has the dirty fingers. Leung knows you. The post office clerk knows your face, and signature. The flight attendant will verify your trips. Soriano has been very clever."

"I know, and I don't want to do this anymore. I'm scared what Frank can do to me."

"Let me think about what we can do, and I'll get back to you shortly. If you hear from Frank, alert me immediately. Tell him you've been ill, or contact Mr. Leung and tell him the same thing. We will catch them both sooner or later. First a word of caution: don't return to Honolulu under any circumstances.

Second, you need a good lawyer."

"My uncle is a lawyer in Oregon. Can he represent me?"

"You need a criminal lawyer, and a local one would be better. Here's the name and phone number of an excellent criminal lawyer in Maui. Get an appointment with him a.s.a.p. You need immunity, and I know Walter Kishimoto, if anyone, can get it for you."

"Thanks, George, appreciate your help," said Joe as he stood up and shook the officer's hand.

A few days later Charlene sat on the Folly with Joe. "I'm so scared. I didn't realize how much of a thug Frank was. I just want to get away from him. Right now, I feel like I'm in a kettle of hot soup, damned whichever way I go."

"Kishimoto should be a good help. Isn't your appointment early next week?"

"He's even agreed to meet me at the plane. I thought he's being very accommodating."

"He's a good friend of George's. They go back a long way."

Moments later Charlene felt a huge tug on her fishing line. "I've got a fish, Joe. Help me pull it in."

"You've got a nice ono on the line. Just hang on, don't let your line slacken, or he'll run away with it. I'll start the motor, and we can take him in closer to shore. That's it, you're doing a great job," he said as he set the motor at a slow speed and limped back to help Charlene with her catch. "It's good to keep your mind in another place. Do you want to fix the ono for us for dinner?"

"For all you've done for me, I'd love to."

Several weeks later, a package arrived at the

Kaunakakai post office. Charlene did exactly as the lawyer and George told her to do. She had a hand-written note to slip inside, and returned the package to Singapore.

Frank, can't make it to Honolulu. Family problems. Returning to Oregon. Can you do it? Sorry. C.

The police kept a watchful eye on who would pick up the package. Undercover police acted as clerks at the post office. As it happened, Frank arrived at the post office himself early one afternoon. He collected the package from the post office box, and immediately hailed a taxi giving the driver Leung's jewelry store address. Undercover police were also waiting at the store, shopping, standing outside smoking. When Soriano entered the store, and sat down with Leung, the police also arrived, at the front and the back doors. Soriano pulled out a gun, but one of the arresting police officers subdued him. Both Leung and Soriano were taken into custody with minimum resistance and transported to the jail for immediate arraignment.

Justice would be swift in this case. Even the FBI became involved because much of the jewelry came from different parts of the world. They were also looking at Frank Soriano because of his involvement in drug trafficking.

"Where's Charlene Harper? She is the one you should be arresting. She's the one who set up the operation." Soriano was vociferous in his claims against Charlene.

"She will be dealt with in due course," said one of the officers.

"I want a lawyer, and you better be damn quick in getting one," he said yelling at the man who undid the handcuffs.

When the case did reach the court docket, Charlene testified. She had been indicted for aiding and abetting Frank Soriano. The fact she blew a whistle on the entire operation was enough for Soriano and Leung to receive a long sentence.

The judge stated to the courtroom, "Charlene Harper, after careful consideration the court has determined you were duped by an unscrupulous man who took advantage of you. For your involvement in fencing this jewelry, you should be given a prison sentence. However, I am putting you on probation for five years. For those five years you will be confined to the islands. If you violate probation, you will go to prison. Understood?"

"Yes, your honor. And thank you for your consideration."

"I will find you a probation officer in Kaunakakai. You will report to him monthly."

Charlene wanted to shout for joy, but constrained herself. "Mr. Kishimoto, I cannot thank you enough." She gave him a spontaneous hug. "George Kapule said you were a good lawyer. I think you're great."

Chapter Twenty

Joe realized Charlene had been target-shooting on her property. He could feel the reverberation, even though he knew she must be using a silencer. When he confronted Charlene one afternoon, her facial features took on a strange look.

"How do you know I've been shooting?"

"I could feel the vibrations. Don't look at me so weird. I just wanted to know if you would like to go hunting again."

"Yes, but no more venison. What can we shoot, now?"

"What about a wild pig? Give us a lot of good meat."

"That sounds interesting. Where can we do that?

"Kaulaupapa has a lot of them roaming around, but there are some around the east end, too, hiding out. We'll definitely need your 'toy' to get there." Joe laughed, and Charlene joined in.

One week later, the two of them were at Misaki's delivering their quarry.

"Enough meat to feed an army for the year," said the butcher. "I give you ham, bacon, pork chops, pork roast. I can even make some sausage for you."

"Whatever we get will be fantastic," Charlene said. "Joe, this was a thrilling day."

Charlene's eyes took on a far-away look.

Next time Joe and I sit at the dinner table I'm going to ask him about a revenge plot. He can take care of Mike, I'll get rid of Leilani. That's what will be fantastic. Out loud, she began laughing.

Joe raised his eyebrows. "Wish I knew what she was thinking," he whispered under his breath.

Chapter Twenty-one

November arrived and so did the Nobles. Cathy helped Leilani with all the necessary plans for refreshments and walked around town with her distributing flyers about the art show. Betty Suguhara had given Leilani a Japanese baby bag for carrying Lia. Strapped over the shoulders, with a nice snug carrying place in the front, Leilani could go with Lia everywhere.

"I can't believe that's how you advertise here," Cathy said, as she thumb-tacked a flyer to a bulletin board outside the grocery store.

"We're a small island," Leilani replied, laughing. The two of them worked in the gallery setting it up to showcase John Noble's work as well as that of Keanu.

That night, Leilani and Keanu sat eating dinner in their kitchen. Keanu had a puzzled look on his face. "How do we keep Charlene away? Ever since her run-in with the law, she's been as quiet as a mouse. This is probably something she would want to come to just for something to do."

"Honey, we can't. We've posted notices all over town about the show. It's open season. I don't think she would do anything in public, especially since George and Jeanie will also be there."

"Well, I corralled a couple of seniors to serve punch and cookies to our guests. I think they will arrive tomorrow late afternoon to help us all."

"I hope they won't break the punchbowl. I borrowed it from the school. Suki from the fabric shop said she would help with the cashiering. Betty Suguhara has three beautiful quilts on sale, and her daughter will be displaying her jewelry. Beautiful silver work, if I do say so myself. I also found a potter who agreed to put his wares up for sale."

The evening crowd swelled till the gallery overflowed with possible patrons. Tourists visiting the island made an appearance also, helping to fill the gallery coffers by their purchases.

The showing was going quite well. Several sales had been made when all of a sudden, a loud shriek pierced the air. "Cathy, Cathy Burke. What are you doing here on Molokai?" It was Charlene hollering at Cathy Noble. "I haven't seen you since junior high school. Do you still live in Pasadena?"

Cathy walked over with a big smile on her face. "You're Charlene Harper. I remember when you moved to Oregon. That was a long time ago. Do you still live there? Are you married? Do you have children?" Cathy peppered her with questions.

"I still own a house in Oregon. I took back my maiden name when I was divorced. And no, I don't have any children, and frankly, don't want any. I love

Molokai, and that is why I'm living here now."

Cathy introduced Charlene to John and the three of them conversed for several minutes. "I left Pasadena when I went to college. John and I met in Europe. See what kind of charm he has. I was smitten from day one."

John interjected. "She still is the most beautiful girl in the world."

Cathy put her arm around his waist and gave him a loving smile. "We spent six months roaming Italy with and without classmates. It was wonderful. Seeing all that beautiful art and having someone special to share it with. We waited until we graduated to get married. John is from Carmel, and since he wanted to carve wood as his artistic profession, we stayed in the Carmel area. I'm teaching school. The reason we were able to come at this time of year was my school had a special week vacation, so we took it. Can we have dinner tomorrow night? John and I will be leaving to return to Carmel the day after that." Plans were made to have dinner the next night at the Molokai Hotel.

Keanu overheard the conversation and repeated it to Leilani after the gallery closed. That's a bit of bad luck, he thought to himself. "She didn't speak with me, and with George there, I don't think she was ready to be cited or arrested."

"She didn't speak with me, either. I saw her looking at the jewelry, so maybe she bought something at that counter."

The Molokai Hotel dining room was filled to capacity. The Nobles were thrilled to be seated where they could see the surf. As the dinner with Charlene progressed, John felt more than uncomfortable, inside he held his seething temper, so he said very little.

"I did a lot of traveling, and wound up in Singapore where I lived for a couple of years," said Charlene. "I reconnected with Keanu. He told me he was moving to Molokai to teach, so I decided to move here also. There's not much to do here for a city girl like me, so I'll be glad when we move back to the mainland." Charlene told the Nobles Keanu had asked her to marry him. He was divorcing Leilani, and moving back to Oregon with her as soon as possible.

Cathy looked at her in disbelief. "Charlene, are you on something? The Emerys are one of the happiest couples I've ever met."

"That's all an act, Cathy," said Charlene. "Keanu is in love with me and will be divorcing Leilani, and we will be moving to Oregon."

"Excuse me?" said John. "I agree with my wife. Keanu is very entrenched here. Are you on pain meds? Your thinking is very cloudy." An angry John became disenchanted with Cathy's old chum from Pasadena.

Charlene bristled. "You can believe whatever you want, John. I know what I'm after and I'm going to get it."

"Charlene, what you are saying seems pretty far-fetched to me. I think Keanu idolizes Leilani." John was shaking his head, first looking at Charlene and then back to Cathy.

"I have my plans. Wait and see."

John stood up from his chair and said loudly, "Charlene, Cathy and I have a bit of packing to do before we leave tomorrow, and I need to make some final arrangements with Keanu for taking his carvings with us."

"You just wait and see what happens, Cathy.

You don't know the half of it."

At that point, John pulled several twenty-dollar bills from his wallet and set them on the table. "This should cover our share, Charlene," he said as he stood up, and pulled Cathy's chair out from the table.

"Amazing to see you, Charlene, after all these years. Take care." Cathy and John rushed out of the dining room and into the parking lot. "John, I think she's loony tunes. I sure don't remember her being like that." They got into their little rental car and sped away down the highway towards the east end.

"John, do you realize you drove in the wrong direction?" Cathy laughed.

"I'm just so pissed at that woman. All I wanted to do was leave." He joined Cathy in laughing. "I think we owe it to Keanu and Lani to tell them about what's going on with Charlene."

"They may already know. But I think you're right. It's not too late in the evening to go knocking on their door."

Ten minutes later the two of them were standing on the Emery's front door step. Lani answered their knock.

"H,i guys, c'mon in. Join Keanu and me in a glass of POG."

"Thanks for the invite," John said as they were ushered inside. "What's POG?"

"The drink of the islands, pineapple, orange, and guava juice. But we doctor it up a bit. You can have your choice, rum, gin, or vodka," Keanu said as he walked over to greet them. "It's so beautiful this evening. We've been sitting outside enjoying the warm breezes." He handed each of them an inviting glass of juice covering ice cubes.

"I'd like some rum added please. Cathy and I wanted to thank you for all your hospitality," began John as the four of them sat comfortably in the cushiony deck chairs. "I know I can sell that beautiful canoe, so we'd like to take it with us."

"I'd be honored, John. Lani and I had a good time with you two, also. And the show was a great success. We plan on doing another one next year."

"We'd like to be a part of it also, if we're invited."

"Goes without saying, John. We just need to get all the dates coordinated. It's probably harder on your part than it is on us. Molokai is so laid back it will only take a couple of weeks to get everything organized."

"We wanted to tell you something."

"What's that?" asked Lani.

"You probably know we had dinner with Charlene tonight. She said some crazy things. Told us you were in love with her, Keanu, always sneaking over to her house for fun and games as she put it. She told us you were just waiting to divorce Lani so the two of you could go back to Oregon."

"She sounds like crazy trouble," said Cathy. "Charlene wasn't at all like that when I first met her, always smiling, always wanting to be helpful. My mom kept telling me my manners should be more like Charlene's. Wait till I tell her what she has become."

"Don't forget, Keanu, when she first got here, how she followed us around in her car and tried to get volunteer work at the school where you are." Lani stood up and put her arms around the back of her husband. "We just wish she would leave. We don't care where. She's on probation with the court. We also have a restraining order against her, but obviously since she came to the art show, she's not paying attention to it. With George there as one of our guests, I doubt she would do anything to cause her to be cited or arrested."

"We just thought you two should know about this evening's conversation," said John. "We're worried for you both. Afraid she might do something to harm you. I would be extra careful, Lani. She's got more than one screw loose."

"While Lani was pregnant, Charlene made a baby quilt, stained it with something red to look like blood, wrapped it and left the package on our front porch. Scared the bejeezus out of us both. She also got into our house one night, and put a picture of her and superimposed me on our refrigerator in a compromising pose. It was such a lewd pose. If Lani went into the kitchen and found it, she could have had a miscarriage. When Leilani screams, it's absolutely blood curdling."

Back at the Molokai Hotel bar, Charlene ordered another drink, pocketed the money from John, and told the bartender her companions had left without paying the bill. She then took different money from her wallet, paid the charges and left. She told everyone, even the shopkeepers in the hotel store what cheapskates her dinner companions had been.

A few days had passed since the departure of the Nobles. Leilani was in the kitchen doing the dishes while Keanu held Lia in his arms, letting her enjoy her nightly bottle. "She's really hungry. The bottle's almost empty. Should we be increasing the amount?"

"I'll ask the doctor when I take her for her checkup. He'll probably put her on solids. Honey," Leilani said, changing the subject, "I really grew to like Cathy and John. And the apartment, it was left in spotless condition. There was no work for me at all."

"Then maybe we should ask them back for two weeks next time, and change the time of the show to coincide with Cathy's vacation."

"Good idea, but the best idea now is to get some sleep. Lia has closed her eyes and we should take advantage of it."

With the lights out, Keanu and Leilani slept in a spoon position. Neither of them moved, until a cry was heard. "It's Lia, she's probably wet. I'll change her." Leilani got up from her side of the bed, and Keanu rolled back over to sleep.

Chapter Twenty-two

For the next several months, Charlene maintained a low profile. She worked in the library, shopped for groceries, and continued to work on her new home. She planted a vegetable garden, and spent a minimum of sixty minutes a day target-shooting with her new rifle. She kept her shooting area a secret from anyone who passed by, including Joe. A silencer on the gun made certain no one could hear bullet noise. Charlene's accuracy improved daily. She traded vegetables from her garden for fish from Joe's catch. Some evenings she cooked a meal for Joe. All the time, she thought about how she could derail Keanu and Leilani's marriage. "It feels good not having to worry about anything except how to get Keanu off the island and back to Oregon," she said to herself.

Pastor Paul accompanied Joe on several fishing trips on the Folly. He could see Joe's physical condition visibly deteriorating, and Paul did what he could to help him. Joe could manage two or three trips a week at the most. Everyone in town saw the changes in Joe, physical appearance as well as attitude. Sobriety became him. He smiled a lot and stayed away from the town bars or the liquor store. Yet thoughts swirling around inside his head did not provide a peaceful aura. Joe still wanted revenge on Mike Palani, and he wanted Malia back in his life. Joe realized Malia would never remarry him, but it didn't matter now. He just wanted Mike out of the picture. Knowing Charlene's feelings about Keanu might be a helpful inroad. As much as Joe smiled, he cared nothing about the children he had fathered or the fact Leilani, his daughter, had married Keanu.

Maybe Charlene and I could combine forces, and get what we wanted at the same time. Good thinking, Joe. Talk to her about it on a hunting trip. Ask her about going one day this weekend.

Joe saw Charlene getting out of her wagon and walked over to the fence to talk to her. "Want to go hunting this weekend?" he asked.

"Can we hunt something besides deer?" she smiled as she answered him. "I still have enough venison to feed an army."

"If this woody of yours can handle rough terrain, we can go after a wild pig again."

"Now that sounds great. Anything particular you'd like in a sandwich besides bologna, Mr. Obregon?"

"Some cheese would taste good. My favorite is Swiss, the kind with the holes in it." He laughed. "Nothing like ordering my own menu. That's real nice of you, Charlene."

Sunday arrived, and with their gear, lunch, and

drinks all stowed inside the wagon, the two of them drove off toward the farthest point on the east end. Joe showed Charlene where to go on a dirt trail that went over the hill to the other side of the island.

"If you hadn't shown me this road, I'd never have known it was here."

"Not many people know about it. If you didn't have four-wheel drive, we could never get here except on foot. We can sit right here in the wagon, and watch for our prey. Do you realize how much ham and bacon and sausage we'll have? I can taste it now."

"Joe, we have to shoot a pig first." She chuckled.

"We will. Look at that bush on your left. There's an animal inside of it. Hopefully it will be our pig."

The two of them sat in silence for another few hours, when they saw movements in the bush again. With as much stealth they could muster, they left the confines of the wagon without shutting the doors, retrieved their rifles and ammunition. A huge ugly black blob came lumbering out of the bush. Shots were fired by both Joe and Charlene. They struck their mark. The wild pig lay still on the ground.

"I think one pig is enough. Don't you?" Charlene asked.

"Yes, I do, but we want to get out of here before the rain starts. While we've been sitting here, the sky has become dark. Hopefully we can get out of here before it starts to pour. Charlene, would you like to have dinner in my kitchen tonight. I caught some ono, and it's too much for me to eat."

"Joe, why don't you let me do the cooking in your kitchen? I've some great veggies in my garden waiting to be picked. Would you mind, if I brought wine for me? If you do, please say so and I will drink water or iced tea."

"No, I can handle it. Please do." This will be a great time for me to see if she is interested in my plan he thought.

Before the two of them returned to their respective homes, they took their prize into town for cleaning and dressing. That evening while finishing their dinner, Joe sat back and looked at Charlene. "Charlene, I have heard gossip around town that you would do anything to get Keanu off this island, and back to Oregon. True or false?"

"It's true. But I still haven't figured out how to do it."

"I would like to do the same to his father-in-law, but I want to make him disappear forever."

Charlene looked at Joe, a malevolent smile crossing her face. "I think we want the same thing. Do you have any ideas for accomplishing this?"

"Every weekend the Emerys go to the Palanis for dinner, usually Sunday nights. I think between the two of us, we could blow out the tires on their car. If one night you were to drop me off somewhere on the highway to Kalae, I could hide and wait for the car to appear, shoot out the tires, maybe some shots at the car. I have a pretty good hiding place. I can take food with me, and you could pick me up a few days later, very early in the a.m. Then you could take my rifle home, and drop me off at the Folly. If I'm fishing early enough, no one will be the wiser."

"That's a brilliant idea. I can pick you up at the dock around three in the afternoon, and drive you home, saying you wanted to go fishing, but couldn't manage the drive and steering the boat all day. How do you propose to get Mike?"

"When Mike is paddling in the canal with George and me. I think you're good enough to manage a long-range shot, put a hole in the boat, and maybe hit Mike at the same time. George and I always wear a life preserver. Mike doesn't. You wouldn't have to kill him. Just wounding him in the leg and arm would make it difficult for him to swim to shore. Maybe he'd make it, maybe not. I'll just have to find you a good place to shoot from. There's a thick grove of palm trees south of here. No one knows you've been target practicing except for me."

"You and your super sensitive ears." She laughed. "You know every time I'm target shooting?"

"I told you I could feel the reverberations every time you took a shot. Special forces can give you a lot of uncanny tools."

Charlene smiled a not-so-nice smile at him.

Chapter Twenty-three

When Paul next saw Joe, he realized Joe's difficulty with balance had become more pronounced. He knew in his heart Joe's physical condition would make it impossible for him to complete his vendetta. *Thank you, Lord. You've answered my prayers.*

The rain poured down on the island. The weather service warned of severe weather, and maybe an impending storm surge. Joe had been fishing out on the Folly. Now he struggled with the boat, hoping to reach the dock without capsizing. He fought with the angry water's monstrous waves. No energy remained in his pain-wracked body. Once he reached his docking space, he took his cane, and with great difficulty, managed to climb over the gunwale onto the dock itself.

Joe hobbled to his truck, afraid he might fall. His truck slogged through driving rain and heavy puddles as he drove towards the east end of the island.

What had been his driveway was now a mud hole. With tremendous effort Joe unlocked his front door and shut it. It took every ounce of strength left in his body to reach the bedroom. Freezing, he shed his wet clothes, dropping them on the floor. He climbed into his bed, pulling all the blankets on top of him, trying to put some warmth into his body. *In all my life, I've never seen rain like this.*

Joe had been lying in bed for about an hour when he heard an insistent noise. Swish, swish, slosh, slosh. *Sounds like it's coming from the kitchen. I'm not getting up to find out.* The noise became more pronounced. Looking over the side of his bed, he saw water on the floor, and more water rushing from the kitchen, through the living room, into his bedroom. *It'll just have to come, I can't do anything about it. Can't move my legs.* The wind blew, and Joe could hear it ripping at his roof. A loud crash confirmed a piece off the roof had been carried away in the wind. Water gushed inside, fast and furious. Joe heard the house creaking. The bones of his house were breaking away from its foundation. He remained completely calm. *I hope Charlene is okay. If I'm going to die, it couldn't be too bad. I came from the sea. Maybe it's just calling me back to its depths. I'm not afraid of Davy Jones.*

The water roiled, aggressive and fierce. A giant wave engulfed Joe's house and everything in it. Joe and his house were swept away.

The next morning was bright and sunny, not a cloud in the sky. No hint that Joe's house ever existed. Everything was gone, even the pilings. Where his house had been was now a vacant canvas. Paul was frantic. He had tried phoning Joe most of the night and early morning.

Paul was in George's office only moments before the police chief arrived.

"George, I haven't been able to reach Joe. Are you going out to that part of the island? If so, I'd like to go with you. I'm really concerned."

"Yes, Paul, I know a couple of aunties living out there alone. I want to check up on them, too. Can you leave now?" Paul nodded in the affirmative.

When George and Paul arrived at the spot where Joe's house once stood, a stunned look covered their faces. They looked towards the land where Charlene's house stood the day before, but it too had vanished in the night.

"Do you think they might have taken refuge somewhere on the island?

"Paul, I don't want you to get your hopes up. That storm was like the wrath of God coming down on us."

"I know. I pray God has been merciful and spared my friend."

The two of them trudged in the mud toward where Charlene's house had been. The thrust of the storm surge even took the foundation where the house originally stood. The high water caused more than considerable damage to the property. Large rocks now studded the entire yard instead of flowers and vegetables. Had Charlene survived? they both wondered.

"Let's get going, George," said Paul as he began to move towards the police car. An icy chill permeated his body.

Several days later George told Paul Charlene's station wagon sat in the airport parking lot. Charlene had been over to the mainland, and returned to find no house and no possessions. She decided to rent a house instead of buying another. Distraught upon hearing about Joe's death, she stayed away from the Palanis, much to the delight of Paul and George.

Chapter Twenty-four

Several years passed since the island had been pounded by the storm. Paul Kanga knew he led a blessed life even though his past had been black and illegal. *I committed a heinous crime to keep the authorities from finding me. My life has been completely changed. I love being a pastor.*

Strange for a man who had a black heart and dealt in drugs for many years. Paul did not miss his old life. He loved being part of a community. He loved his congregation. He missed his friend Joe. Even though much time had gone by, Paul remained concerned Charlene would realize he indeed was Jack Metzger, and would run to George and tell him about his past.

Paul enjoyed helping people and the many friends he had made on the island. He wanted to tell George about his deception but knew his current life would cease to exist. *No matter how much good I have done in the last few years, I'm still a wanted felon.* George had become one of his best friends, not his nemesis, still bird-dogging for clues to identify the body found in the grove pool so many years ago.

One of those many beautiful days seen in Molokai was marred by the news Paul received from his doctor, Kimo Palani.

"Paul, I found a lump in your stomach. I can't tell whether it's benign or a cancer tumor without a biopsy. We don't have the equipment on Molokai for me to perform that kind of surgery. You'll need to go Honolulu as soon as possible. I don't want this hanging over you."

"How bad is it, Kimo? Don't pull any punches on me."

"Paul, truthfully, I can't tell until the surgeon does his bit and studies whatever he finds."

"Well, all that I can pray for is good news."

"Let's hope so. Don't jump to any bad conclusions, Paul." Kimo called the hospital while Paul sat there. "I spoke with a surgeon at Queens Hospital, and he can do the biopsy tomorrow morning. Can you fly out tonight?"

"I'll need to find someone to take over my Sunday service. Even if the news is no good, can I be back here soon?"

"The surgeon will have to tell you that. I can't. We can just pray for the best outcome."

Taking care of finding a substitute for Sunday service, Paul caught the 6 p.m. flight and was at Queens and in pre-op by 9 p.m. The next thing he remembered was waking up in the recovery room, talking with the surgeon.

"Mr. Kanga, it was a cancerous growth, but I think we were able to remove all of it. I'll have the results back in a day or so. In the meantime, I want you to rest. Is there anyone I can call for you?"

"No, I'm just grateful for Kimo's quick intervention. My prayers are answered."

When Paul returned to Molokai, he was greeted by George, who told him about Charlene's latest adventures.

"I thought maybe she would leave the island after the storm, but she stayed on the island, rented another house, and has been more than quiet. She has just taken up a new hobby, though," said George, shaking his head.

"What kind of hobby?"

"She bought a racing motorcycle and now is hanging around in the company of anyone who has one. They've been racing on a stretch of the highway west of town."

"Can't you set down some laws for where or when they can race or not?"

"I've called a meeting of all the motorcycle owners to talk with them about that. Someone or something could get hurt if they race without any kind of supervisory watchdogs, to make certain they don't scare off cars or walkers, or hit an animal."

"Good plan. Even in a place as unpopulated as this island, racing on a main highway could be dangerous." Paul agreed with him.

Charlene seemed to have made herself spokesperson for the group.

"We all love to race. Why can't we have rallies maybe twice a month, regulated by our own race officials? The island can know when and where we're meeting and stay away, or actually come and watch us."

"Here, here," agreed her fellow motorcyclists.

"We might be able to try that," said George warily.

The plan seemed to be working, and the appointed Saturdays or Sunday mornings kept the main highway free and clear for three hours. It was Sunday morning during church service, when Paul's sermon was interrupted by a screeching crash. As the road wasn't supposed to be used for racing at that hour, the entire congregation looked at each other, rose in unison from the pews, and hurried outside to see what had happened. A motorcycle had crashed headlong into a truck and burst into flames as it sailed down the highway at breakneck speed. Another large blast of wind filled the air, fueling the large fire even more. The truck's gasoline tank had exploded. A badly burned truck driver managed to escape from the cab, but the motorcycle rider wasn't so lucky. The co-driver in the truck was dead, and no part of the bike rider's body escaped the fiery inferno. When Paul and George reached the riders, George pulled off a helmet.

"Oh, dear lord, I think Charlene Harper is the other victim. She's the only woman with a motorcycle that I know of."

"She wasn't even racing," commented a witness to the crash.

"What were they doing?" asked one of the bystanders.

"The truck driver must have been on something," said another one. "Has an ambulance been called?"

Several minutes later, a doctor arrived, along with the ambulance. "Let's get this woman to the hospital." To George he said, "I don't think she'll make it."

It shocked the entire town when the coroner discovered the body didn't belong to Charlene Harper. George drove to her home immediately.

"What's wrong, Sheriff?" Charlene said as she opened her screen door.

"We thought you were dead. A woman was killed in a terrible motorcycle crash this morning."

"Oh, my God," said Charlene. "She just asked if she could try out my motorcycle. She told me she knew how to ride one."

"Who is she?" asked George. "We don't have any information in our system on another woman who rides a motorcycle."

"You probably wouldn't. She was visiting me from Tucson. She was thinking about taking a teaching job here. She came to look over the island."

"Do you know if she has any ID in her belongings? I'll need to contact her next of kin and make arrangements for burial or whatever."

Charlene led George into a small bedroom. "That's her suitcase. She had an address book with her. Maybe it's still here. Guess I'll have to call the insurance people about my bike."

George made a cursory glance at the nightstand and saw a small leather book. "I think I found it. Thanks, Charlene." He left the bedroom and walked to the front door.

Chapter Twenty-five

"Ipo, this house is just too small for you and me and baby Malia."

"I know, Keanu. I was thinking Pookie will have to give up her place in the dresser drawer." They both laughed. "Are we going to have to move? I love this place. Maybe the owner would sell it."

"We don't have enough money saved to buy it, and even if we did, we wouldn't have any money to enlarge it."

"Why don't we go talk to Mom and Dad. They know everyone on the island. Maybe they would have some ideas for us. I'll go talk to Mom while you're at school tomorrow."

"Let me think about it, honey," said Malia. I believe the owner would sell. That's not a problem. I'll discuss it with Dad. Why don't you and Keanu come for dinner tomorrow night and we can sort it out?"

"Oh, Mom, that would be perfect. We can be

there around six, if that's okay. Keanu has some team practice in the afternoon, and I know he'll want to clean up before we come for dinner."

The next evening, a beautifully set table greeted Leilani and Keanu.

"We're having fish. They were selling this beautiful akule on Ala Malama. I know you like purple potatoes, Keanu. So does Mike," said Malia as she passed the dish dotted with butter, paprika, and parsley.

"Malia, are you buttering us up, before you tell us what to do?" asked Keanu.

"I just figured what we have to say needs some kind of celebration," answered Malia.

Keanu and Leilani had puzzled looks on their faces. By the time dessert arrived, their stomachs were fidgeting, even though it didn't show.

"All right, children, we don't want to keep you in suspense any longer," said Mike. "But Leilani, this is your mother's show, so I will let her do the talking." Mike smiled at Malia.

"This has to do with an inheritance I was given. I didn't want to keep it, but your Dad said I should. We would know when we had a good use for it. Mike and Kimo don't need it. They have more than enough money to live comfortably. That leaves you, Leilani. We know you and Keanu are struggling to make ends meet, and if you plan more grandchildren for us, we want you to feel safe and secure."

Leilani grabbed Keanu's hand under the table and squeezed it. She wasn't sure what would be coming next.

"Your birth father, Joe Obregon, before he died made out a will at the bank. At his death, I received everything that was in his account plus the property on east island. I went to see the banker, after he called me on the phone. Kimo is the owner of the property on Beach Road."

"But that's not who we dealt with."

"I know, honey, but he's too busy doctoring to take care of real estate. What your Dad, Kimo, and I worked out is this. Kimo will take the property on the east end in exchange for the house on Beach Road. Then you will receive the money in the bank to help you build your home like you would want it."

Leilani and Keanu were beside themselves with joy. They got up from the table and hugged Malia and Mike until their arms hurt.

"Keanu, we really can think about enlarging our house. It's ours now. Can you believe it?" She pinched herself to make certain she wasn't dreaming. "I don't mean to be greedy, but by any chance does my bro' own the small lot next door?"

"Yes, and he already has told your Dad and me that is part of the package."

Leilani just sat in her chair, stunned by all the good fortune happening to her and Keanu within the last few minutes. "If I live to be a hundred, I don't think I could ever be as happy and excited as I am now."

"Lani, I have a friend from Oregon days who is a wonderful architect and builder. I'd love to have him design and remodel our home. Unless there is someone on the island you would rather use."

"I'm happy using your friend as long as he didn't have any connections with Charlene."

"I know for a fact he doesn't. What do you think? He's married, but no kids."

"They could stay in my apartment. How long

do you think he would need to finish it?"

"Just a few months. I'll call him today."

Keanu made a phone call to his friend, and within the month, he and Leilani were sitting at their kitchen table with Gary Tanaka and his wife, Eiko.

"I can see why you want to stay in this location. It's fabulous," exclaimed Gary.

"Lani and I would like to have our studio with lots of windows facing the water. I hope that will be easy to do. We also want to add two more bedrooms and another bathroom. I'd like an outside shower, too, if possible. I guess we can go up if we have to. But I think this lot plus the one adjacent is large enough to keep everything on one floor."

Gary took out his notebook began sketching his ideas. "I think we could turn your living room into a family room, change the entrance to the house, and have the bedrooms come off the family room, two in the front, and the master facing the water."

"But where would our studio be?"

"Off the kitchen, Lani. I'll add a few feet, and take out the wall between the now living room and the kitchen, so you can watch Lia play while you're cooking," replied Gary.

"I like that idea. Has Keanu told you what we'd like to do for lumber?"

"Oh boy, what did I get myself into, my friend? Maybe I should just take the next plane out and return to Portland." He laughed.

"There is such wonderful wood on the island, I would like to go searching for it, cutting down trees where there's no population, and using that wood, not in the framing, but for finished work. Nothing is more beautiful than the wood on Molokai, and I believe beams and other accents would make this house a piece of art, not just a house."

"And how do you plan to get this wood? We're only two men and you have the physique for hard labor. But I don't. I spend most of my time behind an architect's desk."

"I have a lot of able-bodied students who need the exercise for game practice. I think hauling wood would be great for them."

"A challenge you mean?" Leilani entered the conversation. "I think it's a good idea, honey. I really do." She smiled at Keanu and then looked at Eiko. "You told us you didn't want to stay in the apartment, but it's still available if you would like it."

"No, Leilani, I have relatives here. They would be very hurt if Gary and I didn't stay with them. Besides, they're giving me a place to paint," Eiko added.

"I didn't know you were an artist. Did you know I have a gallery downtown? If you finish some work, maybe you'd like to show it there."

"Eiko's very modest," said Gary. "She's an award-winning abstract painter."

"Would you be interested in painting at different spots on the island while our 'boys' work? I'd love to see your work."

"That would be fun. I've never been to Molokai before."

"And I'll take you out to Kalae to have lunch with my mother, and to see the view from the Kauluapapa overhang, and the interesting rock formations."

Elko looked at her puzzled. "Someone told me about a phallic rock? What is it?"

Lani laughed. "Legend has it if a woman touches the rock, she will become very fertile and will give birth to many babies."

"You're kidding?"

"You'll see, Eike, but it's a lovely place where we can hike."

Chapter Twenty-six

Life for Keanu and Leilani continued, but the pace had quickened. Keanu worked hard at school, coaching, then carving in his studio. He loved to play with little Lia, who was growing up too fast, he thought. Leilani interrupted their game Hide and Seek. She had returned from an errand only moments before.

"Keanu, I delivered a painting to the Molokai Hotel, and the person I delivered it to asked about Charlene Harper." It was the weekend, and the time Leilani and Keanu set aside to relax, something they rarely were able to enjoy.

"What? I haven't heard her name in years. I don't even know if she's still in Molokai," said Keanu.

"I think she is. That fancy station wagon she bought years ago is still running. I see it on the road every once in a while. I'll give you a little gossip."

"All ears, beautiful wife." Keanu laughed and pulled her onto the couch next to him.

"Well, the young woman I delivered the painting to lives in Halawa Valley. She told me Charlene had taken up with one of the residents."

"That's hard to believe when she likes the best of everything."

"I'm just glad we are not bothered by her presence anymore."

"I know, but the girl told me Charlene had gone native and as hippie as one could."

"Too much pakololo, I guess."

"I thought she might have told me for a reason. Maybe I'm reading too much into it."

"Let's not talk about my sordid past, ipo. Let's just enjoy the day. We'll have a good time with your parents tomorrow."

Late Sunday afternoon, just as the sun was setting, all the Palanis and the Emerys sat at Malia's dinner table. The table overflowed with native foods—poke, lau lau, kalbe, ribs, purple potatoes, and some green veggies. Akoni and Danh, young men now, planned on heading to the mainland for college in a few weeks. Akoni would be a senior, and Danh a freshman. Brother Kimo had never married, except to his doctoring, which he loved. Grace and Mike both sported a head of graying hair. Grace had brought one of her famous desserts everyone was enjoying when the doorbell rang.

"George, I didn't even hear your car drive up. Come in, come in. Who's that in the car with you? Invite him in too. We're having one of Grace's concoctions." Mike walked back into the dining room with George and his deputy in tow. "You'll find a couple of chairs by the wall, pull them up, and we'll give you some dessert."

"I'm so glad you are all here. Saves me from visiting each of you individually. I'll get right to the point. Have you seen Charlene Harper lately?"

"I thought I saw that old wagon of hers going down the highway towards Maunaloa," Leilani said. "I don't know if she was the driver or not. According to a clerk at the hotel, she's taken up with someone who lives in Halawa Valley."

"That I know," said George. "I talked with him and he told me he and Charlene got into a huge row. He fired a gunshot at her, but doesn't think he hit her. She took off in her wagon, and he hasn't seen her since. That was three days ago. Charlene stormed out of his house and drove off. She's not at her house either."

"That's very strange. Have you seen her wagon after you talked with her friend?" Keanu asked.

"No, but knowing what a crazy lady she is, I'm worried. Someone told me he saw the wagon heading toward Papohaku Beach. The rip tides there have been terrible. I've already had one death reported. Kimo, was that a drowning victim or death by shark bite?" George addressed his question to the doctor.

"Drowning, George. You were just lucky to have recovered the body."

"If I need you, will you come out to Papohoku?"

"Of course I will, George."

Several days later, Kimo received a phone call. "I'll be out there in about one-half hour, George." Kimo grabbed his medicine bag, left his office, and drove to the place where George asked him to meet.

An old woody station wagon sat in the beach parking lot. George had opened the door and searched for some form of registration or identification.

"It's registered to Charlene," he told Kimo. "Obviously, it's been abandoned. No footprints showed in the sand. The tides covered them all."

"Let's walk along the beach, now the tide is low. Maybe we can find some answers," Kimo said. "People should take heed of the warning signs, especially at this time of the year."

The two of them were about to give up their search when Kimo saw a body shape fully buried in the sand. "I think we have our answer. George, help me dig." The two of them recovered a very bloated body with the left leg sporting a gunshot wound to the ankle.

"She's haole," said Kimo.

"It's Charlene. I'm sure of it. I'll call an ambulance and take the body back to the morgue where you can make a complete identification."

The town buzzed with the latest drowning. George checked with the bank to see if she had an account there, or a lawyer listed. In her safe deposit box, he found a document listing the lawyer's name and phone number, George called informing him of the circumstances surrounding Charlene's death.

"Don't do anything 'til I get there. I'll be on the first plane out."

Two days later, a very distinguished looking gentleman with silver hair, wearing a business suit, arrived on the inter-island plane. He took a taxi to the police station.

"I'm Leland Harper, Charlene's uncle and also her lawyer."

"Please come into my office," said George.

"You have to realize how difficult this is for

me. I loved Charlene, but she never seemed right from the time she reached high school. Her parents, my brother, sent her from therapist to therapist. None of it seemed to help. She didn't even come to her parent's funeral when they were killed in a plane crash in the Cascades."

"I knew her parents weren't living, and that she had inherited a great deal of money. We knew about her strange behavior. At one time, court orders existed for her to stop harassing some of our residents."

"I brought her will with me, and you will see how strange she had become. Her bequests are bizarre."

"What do you mean?"

"Just listen."

"I, Charlene Harper, being of sound mind as I write this, will set out the following bequests. I leave all my bank accounts, stock accounts, savings accounts to Keanu Emery with the following conditions. He must divorce his wife and move back to the mainland. I wish to be cremated and have him return my remains to Bend, Oregon, where he will scatter them over Tumalo Falls into the Deschutes River."

"That's absolutely nuts," George said. "Keanu and Leilani have been married for years, and Keanu is going to be the next mayor of Kaunakakai."

"I know it's crazy, but she would never even have a will if I didn't write what she wanted," said the lawyer.

"Keanu will have to go to court," George replied. "That's all I know. Do you want Keanu to come here, or would you like me to take you to his home?"

"Would you take me to him, please?"

Keanu and Leilani were stunned by what the

193

lawyer read to them.

"I told you she was crazy, ipo. If it were all the money the world, I'd never divorce you." Keanu grabbed her hand and held it. "Is there anything we can do?"

"I'll set up a court hearing, and we can petition for a change in the will due to the fact she wasn't of right mind when making or signing this will. It would help if you and Leilani were in court also. I can take affidavits from other people showing her state of mind. It may take a while, but I believe we can get a favorable decision for you."

Court day in Bend, Oregon, came and went. The Emerys returned to Kaunakakai. "I still can't believe I inherited all this money. Ipo, we have to do something with at least part of it. How about repairing the Hawaiian Cultural Center?"

"That's a wonderful idea," said Leilani, "and maybe some money to Kimo's clinic. I can think of all kinds of things. We have time, plenty of time."

Chapter Twenty-seven

It was the day of Malia's birthday, and her family planned a huge celebration at the refurbished Hawaiian Cultural Center. Keanu and Leilani donated money for restoring the beautiful building. It had fallen into disrepair from disuse and neglect over the years. All of Malia's family would be here for the activities, some of them flying in from the mainland. Leilani and Keanu and their daughter Lia were responsible for the festivities. Not even the wheelchair Kimo pushed for his mother could contain the joy she was feeling. Her entire ohana surrounded her. Son Mike, his wife Grace, and grandchildren, Akoni and Danh, now adults with their own families, were greeting everyone as they entered the building.

Kimo stopped the wheelchair for a moment and told Malia to look on the wall. Hanging there was a large painting of Malia. She looked like she had when she married Mike, so many years before.

"I wish Dad were here to see this," said Leilani. She brushed a tear off her cheek and gently hugged her mother.

"I do, too, my darling. When did you have time to paint this?"

"I began a year ago, before Dad passed away. He only saw the beginning sketches but I'm grateful he saw those," said Leilani.

Malia's hair in the painting was coal black with a wreath of plumeria crowning her head. Leilani painted the dress a pale yellow. She had captured her mother's smiling eyes. The background was a beautiful blue sky.

"Mom," said Keanu, joining Leilani, "this painting will hang here as long as the Center remains open. The public will now be able to come here, and visit the small museum of quilts you put together over the years."

Keanu, now the mayor of Kaunakakai, took a microphone and requested everyone's attention. "Malia, you have given so much to this community and this island, we are naming the quilt room in your honor."

Malia smiled. "Thank you, Mr. Mayor, and thank you, people of Kaunakakai. For me, this island is paradise on earth. This is our island of Molokai, where the sign at the airport says, 'Go slow Its Molokai'. Each day the sun rises in the east. The sky is blue, our trade winds soft and refreshing. Our life is simple. Children are born. People die. Each sunset that yellow ball of fire sinks into a momentary splash of emerald green as it disappears over the horizon. This is my Molokai."

Chapter Twenty-eight

One of the many beautiful days seen in Molokai was marred by the news of Paul's physical condition. He began experiencing stomach pains and made an appointment to see Kimo.

"Paul, I found another lump your stomach. You'll have to go back to Queens for another biopsy. I'll call the hospital and see when surgery can be scheduled."

"Can you make it for a Tuesday, so I can be back to preach on Sunday?"

"I'll call you as soon as I have something set up."

"How bad is it, Kimo? Don't pull any punches on me." Paul sat in Kimo's office the following week.

"It's not good. Paul. As much as I hate to be the bearer of bad news, I suggest you put all your affairs in order."

Paul looked at Kimo with a bereft face. "Isn't

there any medicine I could take? How much time do I have?"

"I wish there was something I could do for you, Paul. I'm so sorry. The cancer has metastasized over your entire insides. The surgeon's report indicated more surgery wasn't possible to lengthen your life span. I believe you would rather have quality time, than an extra month added to the few you have left. You probably have three months, maybe four."

A dejected but resolute Paul left Kimo's office that afternoon. He knew what he had to do.

Over the years, Paul had not acquired much in material goods. But he had his congregation that dearly loved him. He had made many friends besides the Kapules, including Malia and Mike Palani, and also Leilani and her husband Keanu. He had a small bank account.

Hopefully that will be enough to bury me. And if anything is left over, my congregation should have it. George will see to it. I know I'm being selfish, but I don't know what else to do. I don't want to die without George knowing the truth about me.

"George," Paul said over the coffee they were drinking in Paul's kitchen at the church. "I need to get a few things off my chest, before I am no longer around. I'm dying."

George's face took on a serious and sad demeanor when he found out his friend's illness had reached the terminal stage. "Isn't there anything the doctors can do?"

"I'm beyond medical help, George. The doctor told me four months at the most. I want to write a letter to my congregation. Will you read it to them after I'm gone?"

"Of course, I will. Paul, I'm at a loss for words."

"Don't worry, my friend. Your friendship has meant a great deal to me."

Once George left, Paul sat at his kitchen table, and tears began to flow. He still had to tell George about his life before Molokai. But a tremendous weight of guilt had been removed from him. He felt almost gleeful when he stood up.

"Thank you, Lord," he said aloud.

Chapter Twenty-nine

Paul did not live the four months the doctor had given him. Kimo told him he would find someone to care for Paul at the end. Paul now lay quietly in his bed. George, who had become his best friend over the years, sat next to him in front of the bedroom window. The nurse had just administered a pain shot to her patient. She smiled sweetly at George with a look that said, "It won't be long now." Many of Paul's congregants stood in the small rectory kitchen praying for their pastor.

"George." Paul opened his eyes. "George," he whispered, "I have a confession. Please don't hate me for what I'm going to tell you. I've done many bad and stupid things in my life. I believe I've atoned for my sin for many years, and I pray God has forgiven me enough for the first part of my life, because I gave him my all for the last."

"I don't understand. You've been a wonderful

pastor, a good friend not only to me but to most of Kaunakakai."

"I have lived under an assumed name for the past twenty years."

George looked at him askance. "What?"

"What I have to say now may shock you, but I hope that you will see the good, and not the bad, since so many years have passed. I came to Molokai from Singapore, being chased by Frank Soriano's goons..."

Telling George the whole story took an hour and all the energy Paul had left.

George paused before saying anything. It was hard to imagine this good man had such a sordid past.

Finally, he said the only thing he could. "Paul, you have done so much for the community of Kaunakakai. I know God has forgiven you."

Paul closed his eyes, feeling relief at his friend's words.

A week later, he passed away peacefully in his sleep. After the service and burial, George opened the letter and read it to everyone.

Dear Friends,

What George is reading to you now may shock you, but I pray you will see the good, and not the bad, since so many years have passed. I came to Molokai from Singapore, being chased by drug dealers because I was involved in a huge drug deal that went bad to worse. The head of the cartel put a contract out on my life, and the only thing I wanted to do was survive. Joe Obregon was a friend of mine in the Navy. He sent me a letter asking for my help in getting Malia away from Mike Palani. He wanted to remarry Malia, and planned to do anything that would allow him to get her back. The night I arrived, I had no money, and a name I couldn't use. My real name was Jack Metzger. The man the Palani boys found in the ocean many years ago was Paul Kanga.

I threw the real Paul Kanga off the cliff and took his identity. He suffered a massive heart attack and keeled over almost at my feet. He was already dead when I checked his pulse. The reason I knew how to preach was that I am the son of a preacher. I was born in Oklahoma in a pure southern Baptist community. Sermons were nothing new to me. I was forced to listen to my father at least twice a week. I knew my way around the Bible. I went to sea when I was seventeen. I ran away from home and lied about my age to enlist. Because my father and I never agreed on anything, I never saw him or anyone else in my family again. I really didn't care because my father was a tyrant. With the war going on, I don't think anyone considered my age. I was not a good man. I managed to stay out of prison even though I did a lot of bad things. God works in miraculous ways because something happened to me on this island. I became Paul from the proverbial Saul. Being a minister gave me a purpose in life. I changed. I wanted to help people."

George Kapule has been the best friend a man could have. I have loved being the pastor of the Good News Church, your church and I pray I have made your lives more meaningful. A new pastor should be taking my place soon. I'm so grateful for the many years I've been able to spend on this island. Molokai became the ohana I never had. May God bless you all.

In Christian love,
Jack Metzger

His congregation and friends cried and sat motionless, wondering how a man whose life had begun in such a sordid way could become a gentle soul. Everyone said the world was a better place because of

Paul Kanga, even if his church life began in an immoral way.

Acknowledgements

Thank you to the people of Molokai who provided me with so much historical information. Thank you from this haole who feels like part of the Molokai ohana. Thanks as well to the public library in Kaunakakai for allowing me access to the old Molokai records. Aloha is truly a way of life, not a word. To Jule Patten Kamakana, artist who provided the kapa for the book cover, and also the chapter heads. All her work is copyrighted so I feel extremely grateful to her for allowing me to use it. Thank you to Clark Dugger for taking the photograph of me. You are the best. To the city of San Diego Coroners Department who informed me about body decomposition in salt water. I'm so appreciative of my Thursday Critique Group who kept me on track to finish Kameleona, and to my editor, Gail Perkins. Finally, but not least, to Marj Charlier of Sunacumen Press for her detail oriented shepherding to bring Kameleona to my readers.

Hawaiian Words

haole: white

hanai: adopted

ipo: sweetheart

huhu: crazy or angry

hale: house

brudda: pidgin English, a word describing friend (like a brother)

ulu: breadfruit

talk story: conversation

kapuna: grandparent, ancestor, older person

kuleana: home site

lolo: crazy

Makahiki: Makahiki Season an ancient Hawaiian New Year's Festival in honor of Lono, the god of agriculture. The holiday covers four months October, November through February or March. The focus of the season is a celebration with athletic games. "Tribal" banners of off-white muslin are decorated with designs draped in a solid color. Crowns of ti leaves and leis of the same are the only adornments of the muscular men in white muslin loin cloths, except for the tattoos the rest of their bodies bear. They bring gifts to Lono of fresh spring water, sweet potatoes, Ti plants, and other crops his followers believe he will like. There is an honoring of the old people. They are escorted to special seats. A horn is heard, and the games begin.

malahini: newcomer

ohana: family

ono: good, tasty, delicious

pupus: food, appetizers

Book Club Questions

1. How do you explain the changes in Paul?

2. What made him a good pastor to his congregation? How do you think he lived with himself knowing all that he had done in his past?

3. Malia was a very strong woman. What more could she have done to alleviate her situation with Joe while they were married?

4. Charlene, the 'fly in the ointment' – what do you think made her tick? Could you feel sympathy for her? No and why? Or yes and why?

5. For Paul, what made Molokai his true ohana?

www.ingramcontent.com/pod-product-compliance
Lightning Source LLC
Chambersburg PA
CBHW021427110726
47901CB00008B/2331